# ACADEMY OF THE FORGOTTEN

CURSED STUDIES BOOK ONE

## EVA CHASE

# CHAPTER ONE

*Trix*

"I'm looking for my brother."

I said the words under my breath as the gate closed behind me, as if I needed to rehearse them—as if the statement hadn't been running through my mind for the entire two days it'd taken me to get here. The wrought-iron bars clanged shut with a finality that made my nerves jump. I glanced back, half expecting to see chains and padlocks had magically sprung up to seal my way out.

The gate still looked as ridiculously foreboding as before, tall and black with imperious twists rising along the arched top, but no unexpected barriers had sprung up. I studied it a moment longer anyway. *Something* strange was going on here at Roseborne College, or I wouldn't have trekked all this way to begin with. But considering how stealthily the strangeness had crept into my life, I couldn't count on concrete proof falling into my lap within thirty seconds of arriving.

The cab I'd gotten out of had already taken off, the growl of its engine fading beyond the thick stone wall. I'd spoken to six drivers before I'd found one willing to come out this far. The college sat at the approximate intersection of No Place Much and Nowhere. I hadn't seen another building along the increasingly sketchy road in at least half an hour.

Gray clouds clotted in the sky overhead. Damp air and a sickly sweet rose scent closed around me. A massive rosebush scaled the wall on either side, the leaves and brambles so tightly intertwined that I could only make out the stones beneath right where they met the gate, but only a smattering of deep red blooms broke the swath of green.

Whatever gardeners they had looking after this place, they were doing a crappy job. A healthy plant would have boasted ten times that many flowers at least. I'd seen more bloom on the sickly little thing I'd nursed back to health in the Monroes' backyard than showed along the entire stretch of wall around me.

Add that to the list of this school's crimes. It'd swallowed up my foster brother, and it abused rosebushes. For a place with "rose" in its name, that should count as two crimes in itself.

I clutched the strap of my backpack, adjusting its weight on my shoulder, and then turned my attention to the building up ahead.

The sprawling Victorian mansion loomed over the vast lawn, three stories of faded red brick and protruding gables. A turret sprouted up haphazardly on one side. It was a far cry from the squat concrete buildings where Cade and I had spent most of our school years, that was for sure.

The image trickled up of watching him make this walk almost a year ago; of sitting rigid in the back of the Monroes' junker Oldsmobile, willing down a cry of protest, while he stepped farther and farther away from me.

And then he'd turned for one last wave with that crooked grin of his, and I'd been socked with a twisted mix of relief and guilt, as hard as if he'd punched me. It wasn't me he wanted to leave, the gesture said. All our plans were still in place.

But only because he had no idea what I'd done.

None of that mattered if I didn't find out what had happened to him since then. I squared my shoulders and marched up the gravel path to complete my mission.

The rose scent chased after me on the cool spring breeze. When I was about halfway across the lawn, the mansion's main door opened, and three figures stepped out onto the porch with a creak of its boards: a guy and two girls, all of them looking to be around twenty like Cade.

One of the girls glanced my way and let out an audible sigh, as if the mere sight of me offended her somehow. It probably did. She was wearing jeans and a scoop-neck top like me, but her jeans were form-fitting and her blouse had the gleam of silk. I was all baggy on the bottom and basic cotton on the top, with a fraying tear across one of my knees. Miss Blondie might also have taken issue with my hair in its current artificial orange brilliance.

Of course, what really made the look were the black combat boots I'd spent months saving up for a few years back as my sixteenth birthday present to myself. They made exactly the right statement: Mess with me and prepare to get stomped on. I was tempted to pull out my matching leather jacket just to see how much more I could horrify her. Or maybe tug up my left sleeve and see if she liked the vine tattoo that decorated my skin from mid-forearm to bicep.

The other two students with her wore posh clothes like hers, the guy in trim slacks and a collared shirt with a starry-sky print that should have looked cheesy but somehow became cool because of the confidence in his stance. The same confidence turned his quirky looks attractive rather than just interesting. His nose had a small bump to it as if it'd been broken and never set quite right, and his square chin should have been a little much for his otherwise soft jaw, but it was hard to imagine any combination of features working better than those did.

He said something to the girls with half a smile and swiped his hand through his light cinnamon-brown hair when they twittered. As he ambled toward me, his eyes narrowed.

"Why don't you turn around and head right back out while the getting's good?" he said in a coolly nonchalant voice, motioning toward the gate. "You don't really think anyone here is going to want you around, do you?"

Interestingly attractive and a total jerk. What else

should I have expected at a school so exclusive no one I knew had ever heard of it before Cade's scholarship offer had shown up in the mail?

I cocked my head and narrowed my eyes right back at him. "You don't really think I give a shit what you want, do *you*?"

He shrugged, seemingly unfazed. "I'm just saying you're wasting your time. Whatever you're looking to get out of this place, it's not here."

"Somehow I'd rather not just take your word for that," I informed him, and marched on by.

The girls murmured to each other as I passed them. I only caught the words "never learn" and nothing else. What did they even think I was here for? Was their hostility simply because I didn't fit the typical new student vibe and that pissed them off? As if I even wanted to be here at their gothic nightmare of a school.

I tramped up the porch steps and across the creaky boards to the front door. It swung open at my tug. With a clench of my jaw, I stepped into the dim space on the other side.

The massive foyer was lit by a large, circular chandelier gleaming overhead, but the dark wood paneling that covered every wall sucked up that light. A crimson-and-gold Persian rug sprawled several feet across the polished floor to a broad staircase. On either side of its base gleamed matching suits of medieval armor, massive shields braced in front of them. The stairs split at a landing halfway up and veered off in opposite directions toward separate wings of the building.

On the first floor, arched doorways led to first-floor hallways beyond the staircase; another doorway at my right opened into a sitting room with a cluster of Victorian sofas, although no one was sitting in there right now. At my left, a closed door held a brass sign etched with the words *Main Office.*

The rose smell had followed me inside. Here, it was cut by a hint of something stale, like old clothes that had been shut away in an attic for decades. My nose itched with it.

I turned and rapped on the office door, figuring that was my best starting place.

A tall, almost spindly man answered my knock. He peered down at me over his hooked nose with piercing blue-gray eyes, his silver hair slicked back from his forehead as solidly smooth as if it'd been sculpted onto his head. Even his pale skin had a silver sheen to it, as if his advancing age had started to leach all the color out of him from head to toe. His dark gray suit matched perfectly.

"How can I help you, Miss…?" he asked in a dry, gravelly voice.

"Beatrix Corbyn," I said, figuring from experience that my full name would go over better with the school staff than my preferred nickname. I had to care what they thought at least a little if I was going to get answers. "I'm looking for my brother."

The declaration had felt much more momentous when I'd pictured making it before. In reality, the words simply faded into the air, and the spindly man continued peering at me, a puzzled line forming in the middle of his forehead.

"He got a spot here on scholarship," I went on. "Cade Harrison? He came at the end of August last year."

The man shifted his weight, and I got the impression he'd have liked to close the door in my face. Instead, he nudged it a little wider and stepped back.

"Why don't you come in and I'll see what I can tell you? I'm Dean Wainhouse, and all student affairs at Roseborne College fall within my purview."

I didn't know what exactly I'd been expecting from the school office, but it definitely wasn't the room I stepped into. It held a big oak desk surrounded by bookshelves at one end and a sitting area with a sofa and armchairs around a fireplace at the other. No secretaries, no filing cabinets, no computer stations—none of the typical features I'd become familiar with during my many trips to various offices across elementary, middle, and high school.

Apparently the dean handled his own paperwork and scheduling. If there was any paperwork. He positioned himself behind the desk, but he didn't take anything out of the drawers or any books off the shelves. You'd have thought the guy believed any information he needed to know would absorb into him by osmosis just by standing there.

I stayed on my feet too, liking the feel of my boots' thick soles supporting me, and waited to see what he'd say next.

His stare shifted to gaze off into the distance beyond me. "Last August, you said?"

"Yes. Our foster father drove him out here. I came along to see the place." To see Cade off. I'd thought it was only going to be for a few months, until Christmas at the very most. Since we'd been thrown together three foster homes and twelve years ago, we'd never been apart even that long before.

"Very strange." The dean frowned. "I don't recall a student by the name of Cade Harrison. Are you sure it was Roseborne he came to and not one of the other private colleges in the state?"

"Yes," I said. "Like I said, I was here. I saw the place." And how could he be so sure whether Cade had been enrolled without looking at a single record?

But even as I spoke, a worm of doubt wriggled into my mind. When I'd gone searching for the scholarship documents to confirm the school's address, I hadn't been able to find a trace of them. The Monroes had stared at me in bewilderment when I'd asked them about the college.

Of course, they'd also looked totally befuddled when I'd mentioned the drive out here and the fact that Cade was missing at all. Our foster mother's voice came back to me with a fresh chill. *Cade? What are you talking about, Beatrix? You were alone when we took you in—and it hasn't been hard to see why. We've never fostered any boys.*

Like he'd never existed. But I *knew* I hadn't made up twelve years of memories. I couldn't have simply imagined the most important person in my entire life, the only person I'd ever been able to count on. Even if all the photos I'd had of us together had vanished from my phone and my computer. Even if none of the mutual friends I'd talked to had so much as recognized his name. *Cade? Um, no, haven't known anybody named that. Why do you look so serious about this, Trix? You sure you're all right in the head?*

All I'd gotten as I'd tried to understand what was going on was confusion, skepticism, and laughter. But I could still feel the ghost of Cade's hand knuckling my shoulder when he teasingly gave me a hard time. The coppery scent of his skin when he pulled me close. There was no way I could have made all of that up… right?

I'd been here. I'd known the bramble-choked walls, the wrought-iron gate, and the looming mansion the moment I'd seen them. This was the last place I was sure my brother had been. Whatever had happened to him—and to everyone who'd known him other than me—the trail started here.

Unless he'd been completely erased from here too, with no trail left to follow.

Unless I *was* going crazy, and he really hadn't existed at all.

"I really am sorry I can't offer more," Dean Wainhouse said. "It is a tight-knit school. I'm generally familiar with all our students."

I dragged in a breath. I'd only just gotten here—I wasn't going to roll over just like that.

"Can I stick around for a little while?" I asked. "Talk with some of the students, see if anyone remembers seeing him back then?" It was possible something had happened to him before he'd even started classes.

The dean's expression gave me the same feeling as when I'd thought he was going to close the door on me, but after a moment he nodded. "All right. As long as you don't interfere with their studies. Please don't enter the classrooms or interrupt anyone who's at work."

"That's fair. Thank you."

I slipped out of the office, trying to ignore the sinking sensation in my stomach. What if no one here could tell me anything? What if all the other students were pricks just like the ones I'd encountered outside?

*Where the hell are you, Cade?*

The foyer was still empty. I wasn't sure which halls led to classrooms and which to whatever leisure rooms the college offered. In the absence of a clear direction, I wandered toward the nearest doorway to the left of the grand staircase.

The wood-paneled wall there held seven painted portraits, all the same size and in the same gold-flecked frames. I stopped for a second, eyeing them. From the rectangle of faded varnish at the end of the row, there'd used to be eight. The strange thing, though, was none of the figures were elderly school patrons or former deans or what have you. All seven of the portraits appeared to be of older teens—three girls and four guys.

They all stared straight forward, wearing the same uniform of white dress shirt and burgundy jacket. The paintings had been done in totally different styles, though —some watercolor, some acrylic, some oil, and obviously by different artists. One was so detailed I'd have taken it for a photograph from a distance; one verged on abstract with its bold colors and blunt lines.

Other than the particularly detailed one, they were

decent but amateurish enough that I couldn't imagine they'd been professionally done. Maybe it'd been a self-portrait project from art class, and these seven had been held up as the best?

I was about to walk on when my gaze caught on a mark at the bottom right of one of the girl portraits—where you'd expect the artist's signature to be. My breath caught in my throat. I stepped closer, my left hand rising to touch my right forearm.

It was a signature, just not in any way most people would have recognized: a little white starburst, slightly uneven with the top tines a little longer than the bottom ones. It was *Cade's* secret signature, modeled after the pale starburst birthmark just below his left elbow. I had a nearly identical mark on my right arm, like a mirror image, where I'd carved it with one of our then-foster father's hunting knives when I was eleven and Cade was twelve, as a promise that our lives were meant to be one and the same.

My hand trembled as I reached out to hover my fingers over the symbol on the painting, but my lips curved into a smile. Now that I'd noticed the symbol, I could sense Cade's presence in the energetic strokes of the stark acrylic colors. He wasn't an artistic prodigy, but he'd brought a vigor to the image that made up for its flaws.

It didn't matter what the weirdo dean or the jackass students said to me. He'd been here, just as I remembered him. I had the proof hanging right in front of me.

So where was he *now*?

# CHAPTER TWO

*Trix*

I backed away from the painting with Cade's starburst signature and nearly bumped into a guy I hadn't heard coming up to me.

"Hey there," the guy said, catching my elbow just before it jammed into his ribs. He shot me a flash of a smile to show he took no offense and released my arm gently by my side. "You look a little lost. New to the school?"

Apparently not all the students here were total pricks. This one was what back home I might have dismissively called a "pretty boy": features so soft they were almost androgynous, intense golden-brown eyes, silky straight hair that fell to just below his ears. But the smooth black strands were shot through with punk-bright green, a silver ring pierced the end of one of his arched eyebrows, and over the top of his khaki-green cargo pants, his deep purple sweatshirt was screen-printed with a bold scarlet tiger. Clearly not so soft after all.

Maybe he was another scholarship student—which might mean he'd have been more likely to have talked to Cade. A jolt of hope shot through me.

"Sort of," I said. "I'm not actually going to be attending classes or anything, but my brother was. He started here back at the beginning of the school year—I'm trying to find out if he's still on campus, or if not, where he might have gone."

If the guy thought my dropping in out of the blue was weird, he didn't show it. His voice came out mellow if a bit hoarse. "I might be able to give you a hand. What's his name?"

"Cade Harrison. About this tall." I held my hand half a foot over my head. "Blond hair. Would have dressed more like you or me than the posh kids. He was here on scholarship."

The guy rubbed his jaw. "Cade... I don't know. That doesn't ring any bells for sure. But we can take a look around if you want some help."

My spirits deflated with his response, but I couldn't see how it'd hurt anything to have a tour guide if this guy wanted to offer his services. I'd at least work my way through the school faster that way. "All right. The dean said I can talk to whoever I want as long as I don't bother anyone in class or doing schoolwork. I was going to head down that way." I pointed to the hall.

"That's a perfectly good place to start." The guy raised his hand in belated greeting. "I'm Ryo, by the way."

"Trix," I said. "Short for Beatrix." I fixed him with a look stern enough to convey that if he tried to make use of my full name, he'd regret it.

"Trix. Excellent. Let's see what we can find." He gave me another smile, but at the same time his eyes crinkled at the corners in a way that gave his expression an unexpectedly melancholy cast.

That solemn impression vanished as Ryo switched into easygoing tour-guide mode. "The first floor has most of the professors' rooms and the non-educational common areas," he said, and pointed to the first room beyond the doorway. "Dining hall."

A few students were sitting at the eight-seater wooden tables inside, one of them gnawing on a muffin, the others using the space for some midday reading. I guessed that would probably count as the sort of schoolwork the dean had ordered me not to interrupt.

As I glanced inside, a couple of the inhabitants looked up. At the sight of us, one made a slight grimace and the other turned back to her book with a roll of her eyes. The overall student population seemed to have a grudge against newcomers. Maybe I needed to wear a sign with flashing lights saying, *I'm only here until I find my brother.*

Ryo nudged open the next door down to reveal a space full of ceramic countertops, antique appliances, and shelves of pots, pans, and dishes. A guy was clattering silverware in a sink full of soapy water; two girls across from him were assembling sandwiches on wooden cutting boards. They already had a stack of at least a dozen on a platter.

"Kitchen," Ryo said, as if that wasn't obvious.

"The students do the food prep and cleaning?" I asked. Or maybe the college had a culinary program—although I didn't see a teacher overseeing this bunch, and sandwiches were hardly high cuisine.

Ryo nodded, his green-and-black hair swinging with the motion. "We handle pretty much everything around the building—cooking, cleaning, laundry. It's all assigned in shifts. You get used to it pretty fast."

I'd never heard of a college, let alone an uber-exclusive one, where the attendees also functioned as the housekeeping staff. So much for their snobby airs. Did the girl who'd given me that disdainful sigh wash dishes in her silk blouse and tailored jeans?

"I guess it's a pretty small place overall," I said. Maybe it simply wasn't practical to try to house a full staff when the students could pitch in.

"Well, you've only seen one part of it." Ryo moved on down the hall. "Exercise room," he said in reference to a space with a mat-covered floor and weights stacked in one corner. A guy's muscles bulged as he did a standing press with a large set. Across from him, a girl was hopping from one foot to the other over the whirl of a dingy-looking jump-rope.

"Hey," Ryo called out casually, as if breaking their workout concentration was no big deal. "Either of you remember a guy named Cade Harrison?"

The guy's gaze flicked to us and then away again with a brusque shake of his head. The girl didn't slow her rhythm.

Her lips pursed as if the question annoyed her. "Can't help you."

That didn't mean she knew nothing, I couldn't help noting, only that she didn't feel like sharing what she knew. I eyed her for a moment before following Ryo onward.

We passed a closed door to what Ryo said was the infirmary, an empty music room with shelves of instruments along the walls, and a smaller space lined with clothing racks that I guessed was costuming for some sort of theater department, although Ryo simply called it "the wardrobe." Before I needed to say anything, he asked the girl who was pawing through the racks if she knew anything about Cade. She waved us off with mild irritation. When I glanced back at her, I thought I caught a glare just before she jerked her gaze away.

Was answering that question really that huge of a nuisance? A creeping sensation was starting to spread over my skin.

Even Ryo's attitude took on a small but noticeably impatient flavor as we emerged back into the foyer. He flicked his hand toward the righthand hallway. "Nothing down there except teachers. If the dean couldn't help you, they won't either. Come on. Classrooms are on the second floor, dorm rooms on the third."

As we headed up the stairs, I studied him more carefully than before. Why was *he* being so helpful, anyway? I'd thought maybe he'd been happy to see someone whose attitudes, at least about personal grooming, aligned more with his than those of the other students I'd encountered so far. But I was getting the feeling that he'd already decided this quest wasn't going to lead us anywhere, so he was ushering me through the tour and the questions as quickly as possible without overtly rushing.

If he didn't actually want to help, what was he after? In my extensive experience with people who hid their real intentions, the truth was never anything to rejoice about when it came out.

I also had plenty of experience at dodging people who were out to use me somehow. Whatever his ulterior motives might be, he wasn't going to find me an easy target.

The second floor hallway wrapped right around the open space over the stairwell, amber light streaming from a second chandelier. There were three classrooms on each side and a massive set of double doors at the far end that led to a library full of books that all looked—and smelled, even from the threshold—at least a hundred years old. It held no seating, only the built-in shelves on every wall and a few rows of them down the middle too, so I wasn't surprised that no one wanted to hang out in there.

I wasn't going to barge into any of the classes after Dean Wainhouse's warning, but as we left the library, a group of students came walking out of one of those rooms. Really, trudging was a better word for it. They all appeared to be the age I'd expect at a college, somewhere between late teens and early twenties, but their faces... The best word I could use to describe them was *haggard*. I wouldn't have been surprised if one of them had pitched themselves over the railing in an attempt to end their apparent misery.

"What godawful class did they just have?" I murmured to Ryo. "It must be brutal."

My tour guide's gaze skimmed over his peers with a glazed quality, as if he'd rather not consider them too closely. "Could be anything," he said in the mellow tone he'd used throughout this tour. "The teachers can get into a demanding mood sometimes."

Demanding didn't seem as if it'd wear an entire class down that much, but maybe we had different definitions of demanding. I debated approaching one or two of the students before they drifted away and asking about Cade, but the glance one of the girls shot my way, as if she knew I was considering hassling her and would sooner commit seppuku than have to listen to my questions, held me back for a second.

In that second, Ryo took the questioning upon himself. "Anybody know where a guy named Cade Harrison is at these days?" he asked the hall at large.

We got a bunch of shaken heads and disgruntled mutterings in response. I sucked my lower lip under my teeth and resisted the urge to nibble at it. Was there really no one here who remembered him—had he been wiped out of existence at the school just like he'd been back home?

But his signature was still on that painting. He hadn't been completely erased. I couldn't shake the impression that *someone* here must know more than they'd been willing to say so far. There was something weird about the way certain students had looked at me, as if they could guess what I wanted to ask—and dreaded it. Maybe they didn't like newcomers, especially ones decked out like I was, but that didn't totally explain the reactions I'd gotten.

Let's be real. The whole college had a weird vibe. So far I hadn't seen any reason at all why someone who had options would go here. The letter and the brochure Cade had gotten had talked about elite professors, unique programs, and "connections that would last a lifetime." I guessed all that could be true and the place could still be drearier than a shriveled bouquet by a gravestone, but my doubts were growing by the second.

I had to admit that didn't mean anything at the school was responsible for his bizarre disappearance, though. None of that made any sense. I couldn't even imagine telling Ryo why I'd insisted on taking the trip out here, why I was so sure something was wrong, because of how crazy I'd sound. For all I knew, Cade had spent a couple of days here, felt just as skeptical about it, and taken off— and run into much deeper trouble wherever he'd gone next.

I might not be able to explain why I was so worried about my brother to Ryo, but maybe he could help me understand why anyone stayed here at all. I turned to him. "How did you end up going to school here, anyway?"

He leaned back against the railing, elbows askew. "Scholarship like your brother. It was an offer I couldn't refuse. And, well, it was a chance to do something different from the path I'd been on before."

"Do you *like* it here?" No one I'd seen so far had

looked all that happy.

He laughed. "I don't think many people go to school mainly to have fun. I've learned... a lot." That hint of melancholy passed over his face again, tightening the edges of his mouth for just a second before it vanished. "It's where I'm meant to be, so obviously everything worked out fine."

I would have pushed harder in one direction or another, but he was already moving, sauntering over to the narrower side halls that branched off from the classroom area. Two much less grand staircases rambled up toward the third floor at either end.

"All you'll find upstairs are the bedrooms. Girls in the south wing and guys in the north. Five rooms with six people in each, if they're all full up. You're not allowed on the guys' side, but I can ask around for you and report back."

Would he? He made the offer so easily. The suspicions that had risen up earlier sent a prickle down my back. I glanced toward the stairs that he'd gestured to at my right. "Sure. I'll go up and see if any of the girls know about Cade."

"I'll find you sometime after, then," Ryo said, without any indication that he was worried about our paths crossing. He raised his hand in farewell. "We'll figure this out, Trix."

He didn't even know how huge a mystery I had to unravel. The truth was, as friendly as he'd been acting, I was alone here just like I'd always been when Cade wasn't by my side.

That was fine. No one to piss me off. No one to piss *on* me. I had way less to worry about that way.

The staircase led to an even smaller hallway with a dormer window over the stairs, two doors on either side and one at the far end. I knocked and then eased open the unlocked door closest to me, and found the cramped bedroom on the other side empty.

As Ryo had said, there were six beds—twins in simple wooden frames—along the walls, each with a bedside table that must have been for personal belongings and a low chest underneath where the students must keep their clothes. The walls held no décor, but from a jacket slung over a bedpost there and a plate left on a bedside table there, I could determine that all of those beds had residents.

I tried each of the other four rooms in turn, making my way down the hall. In the second one, a girl was lying under the covers of one of the beds. I closed the door quickly without taking any more time to look around. The third and fourth were both empty, only five of the beds in each showing signs of occupation. Like with the first, the walls were bare, the furnishings basic—no sign that anyone had tried to make the space at all homey.

Was that a college rule? No wonder the students were depressed if they had to spend the whole school year living like this.

As I stood in the doorway to the fourth bedroom, my mind slipped back to the day I'd been dropped off at the house belonging to my second foster family—the Fricks. When the social worker had brought me around for an initial visit a few days before, the smiling wife had shown us a small but bright bedroom that was supposed to be mine. As soon as the door had closed behind me and my duffel bag on my official arrival, I hadn't gotten anything but frowns. She'd led me down to a chilly, cement-walled basement room with four metal cots and a creaky dresser each of their four fosters got one drawer in.

My first placement had been crappy too, so I wasn't really surprised, even at seven years old. When your parents cared more about getting their next meth fix than making sure you were getting a single square meal a day, and the generous folks who took you in next had a sport of seeing who could cause the most pain without leaving any visible marks any time you annoyed them, you have to be *really* dim not to figure out that someone being a grown-up meant shit-all about whether they were going to look out for you.

I couldn't completely hate the Fricks, though, because they'd brought me and Cade together. I'd been standing there in the cold room, clutching my bag and gathering my fortitude, when he'd come breezing in: tow-headed and scruffy with dirt and bits of grass from working in the front yard, all of eight but with ash-gray eyes as bright as if they contained decades of fiery energy smoldering beneath.

"So, they got you too, huh?" he said, looking me up and down with a sympathetic grimace. "They're assholes, but you'll be okay once you get used to it. Just stick with me, all right?"

Just like that, I'd felt *safe* for the first time in years.

And that was the beginning of everything.

My fingers tightened where I was gripping the door handle. I couldn't let *this* be the end. He'd been there every time I needed him, and sometimes when I hadn't even realized I did. I couldn't stop until I reached him.

That thought was running through my head when I stepped into the last of the bedrooms at the end of the hall. A dormer window high on the wall let sunlight stream over the six beds in their now-familiar configuration. A girl with a dark cloud of curly hair was sitting on one, her back mostly to me, her pen scratching as she wrote something in a notebook. Like the previous two rooms, I spotted one bed that was totally bare of any personal belongings, the top of its bedside table hazy with dust. Resolve rose up to grip my chest.

"Hey," I said. "Is anyone using that bed?"

The girl glanced over at me when I pointed, and my stomach lurched at the sight of her face. One side—the side I'd seen a sliver of when I'd come in—was regular olive-toned skin, smooth other than a sprinkling of faint acne marks on her cheekbone. But a rippled line cut across her forehead and nose and down her other cheek, touching enough of her mouth to pull that corner down with the patchwork of scars that spread out all the way to her hairline and neck.

They looked like burns, mottled pink from pale to vicious, in some places raw red as if they hadn't totally healed yet. Her right eye, lost in that mess, squinted under a lumpy eyelid. She stared at me defiantly.

I held in my shock as well as I could and forced my

lips into a stiff smile as I gestured again. "Sorry to bother you. I just wondered if that bed is free."

"No one's using it," she said in a clear, almost melodic voice that didn't fit her rough appearance at all. Then she turned back to her writing.

The rapping of shoes with sturdy heels carried up the stairs. When I glanced back, a middle-aged woman with a heap of cocoa-brown hair piled on top of her head was striding down the hall toward me. She came to a stop, lifting her thin nose with such an air of authority that I immediately pegged her as one of the teachers. The dim light in the hall gave her skin an ashy pallor.

"I'm going to have to ask you to leave," she said, clipped and nasal. "The dorms are our students' private space."

The scarred girl made a noise that might have been a muffled snort. The woman in front of me ignored her.

I crossed my arms over my chest. "I'm not ready to leave. Something happened to my brother here, and I can't go until I know where *he* went."

The woman let out a huff. "I'm sure you're mistaken. If you'll follow me—"

"I'm not," I said firmly. The idea that had tickled up in the back of my head a minute ago reasserted itself. If it was a strange request, oh well. Everyone and everything here was strange enough to handle that. "There's a spare bed in this room. I'd like to stay, just until I figure out what happened. I'll pitch in with the chores and everything the students do while I'm here—I can earn my keep."

She eyed me for a long moment. "That would require the dean's permission. Admission at Roseborne comes by invitation only."

"I'm not asking to be admitted as a student," I said. "I can stay out of the way of anything to do with the actual classes."

"I'm afraid that wouldn't be acceptable. Our approach to education only works if all participants are fully committed."

The way she said those words sent a shiver over my skin with the memory of how that one group of students had looked as they'd come out of the classroom downstairs. I still wasn't sure what the hell kind of classes they taught here anyway. What kind of weirdo policy was that—to say anyone staying on the premises had to become a student, whether they were qualified to attend or not?

But really, how bad could things be? Strangeness aside, it was a college, not a torture dungeon. And in the past nineteen years, I'd survived plenty of torture as it was, not to mention plenty of classes I'd had no plans to get invested in.

I shrugged. "Let's go ahead and see if the dean will agree to it, then."

If Dean Wainhouse refused to give permission, well, they'd have to drag me off campus kicking and screaming, and then I'd march right back through the gate. I'd clamber over the fucking wall if I had to. I'd come here for a reason, and no amount of haughty stares was going to make me back down from it now.

# CHAPTER THREE

*Jenson*

I'd be lying if I said laundry duty was my least favorite job around Roseborne College, but it couldn't have been much lower on the list. The ancient machines sputtered and groaned through every load of sheets and towels like a kraken awaking from the deep. It was probably a miracle they worked at all. The fabric came out of the washing machines heavy, wet, and chalky-smelling, and then out of the dryers with a flood of rose scent that must have seeped through the ventilation.

Everything in this damned place smelled like roses. My nose had adapted enough that I could ignore it most of the time, but the flood that washed over me when I heaved the linens out of the dryers made my gut clench.

This morning's duties were worse than usual. This morning, Trix Corbyn was scheduled to the same shift as me, taking turns hauling baskets down from the upper floors and folding the stuff once it'd run through the gauntlet. It seemed like no matter where I looked, her orange hair was blazing at the edge of my vision. It sent a stinging sensation through my chest, as if scraping at a cut inside me that had only just started scabbing over.

I didn't want her here. I didn't want her anywhere near me at all. We'd both be better off if she got the hell out of here and never looked back. She shouldn't have ended up at Roseborne in the first place, and it sure as hell wasn't going to get any kinder to her now that she had.

It would've been a lot easier to convince her of that if she hadn't been so fucking stubborn. Telling her off when I'd first seen her clomping her way toward the school hadn't done a thing. I'd spent most of my life figuring out what made people tick so I could sway them into doing what I wanted, but this girl was a design all of her own.

Which maybe was part of the reason my gaze kept sliding to her, garish hair aside.

I had to take my opportunities when they came. I sidled over to her at the folding table and grabbed a fitted sheet to wrestle with.

"So, you liked it here so much you decided you'd nab a spot that should be someone else's?" I said in an offhand way, with just enough edge to needle her.

She glowered at me for only a second before going back to her stack of towels. "No one was using that bed. And I'm not planning on staying very long."

"How do you know the administration wouldn't have offered it to someone else? And thinking it's okay to take it when you don't even care enough to stick around?" I tsked. "Why not save us the trouble and take off now to get on with whatever more important things you have to do?"

I felt the misstep in my last sentence even as it was coming out and restrained a wince. I'd put on a lot of fronts in my time, but overt asshole wasn't one I'd ever had much use for. Obviously that persona needed more work.

"The most important thing I could be doing is what I'm already doing right here," Trix said tartly, not even bothering to look at me this time.

So much for getting under her skin. I'd only reminded her of her cause. As if she had any real hope of seeing it through. This place would chew her up before it let her get anywhere with her private mission.

She dropped the last towel on the top of the pile and moved to heft them off the table. "Of course," I shot back while I still had the chance, letting my tone go dry with sarcasm. "We'd never survive without your stunning laundry skills."

Trix didn't even bother to respond. She marched over to the bins, set the towels in one, and wheeled that out of the room without a backward glance. But I caught a glimpse of her face as she straightened up, of the twitch of her jaw and the momentary knitting of her brow before it fell away behind her tough-girl façade.

She wasn't hard all the way through. Lord only knew how much sadness and confusion lurked under there that even I hadn't seen. She could put on all the fronts *she* wanted, but you couldn't bullshit a bullshitter. I knew every gambit there was.

"And here I thought we had the privilege of being specially chosen for this fine establishment," I said to the room at large after she'd left. "Whatever will we do if word gets out that just anyone can wander in and claim one of these golden spots?"

The wry remark earned me the snickers I'd been aiming for. My life here was a hell of a lot easier if no one else saw me as a total asshole. Self-mockingly charming jerks, on the other hand, got a pass almost every time.

There'd been a long time when that thought would have brought a satisfied smirk to my face, at least when no one was watching. Now, it poked a deeper hole in the pit of my stomach.

That was who I was. That was why I was here. What was the point in pretending any differently? It wasn't as if I could really hurt anyone around me, not anymore.

"Ugh, I'm so tired of doing this crap," one of my fellow inmates said, stumbling under the weight of the heap of damp fabric she was attempting to move from one machine to another.

I tossed the sheet I'd been grappling with aside—someone else could deal with the fitted monstrosities—and caught the mountain of blankets before they tumbled onto the floor. "Tell me about it. Here we go."

We hefted it together into the dryer and closed the lid with a clang. The girl I'd rescued smiled at me as she reached for the dial to start the cycle. "Thanks, Jenson."

I gave her a jaunty salute. "How can I leave a fair maiden in distress?"

It'd been way too easy to bring that blush to her

cheeks. Another jab of discomfort ran through my stomach as I turned back to the folding table. Michelle was pretty, don't get me wrong. But my time at the college had drained away most of my lustful spirit like it had so much else. It was hard to look at any of my classmates without seeing the broken soul beneath the surface.

Hardly anyone liked to talk about why they were here, but after enough classes, you could put together the pieces. Fuck-ups, all of us.

Except Trix. The school hadn't claimed her—she'd claimed the school. At least at first. As much as I'd have liked to see someone saunter out of here giving the brick walls and the fucking roses the middle finger, it'd be hard to believe it was possible until it actually happened.

And she didn't seem to be inclined to try just yet. How many kicks in the ass would it take?

With that question running through my head, I'd girded myself to offer more heckling by the time she ducked back into the basement room, this time with a bin full of towels and cloths from the kitchen. She'd wrinkled her nose—those loads always stunk to high heaven.

"I'd almost think you like the drudgery," I said. "Are you so eager to fit in you'll truck around dirty laundry just to be around us?"

She shoved the bin over to the washing machine Michelle had just emptied. "I told you, I've got something important to do here."

"So why are you doing all these other things instead? I think you're stuck, and you just don't want to admit this was a dead end."

Her gaze jerked to me, startled, but it wasn't as if word about her search hadn't spread all over school by now, especially with that dork Ryo championing her cause.

"You don't know anything about me," she snapped, which told me this time I'd landed the blow.

Hurray for me. I found I couldn't think of any way to build on my "victory" while she tossed the contents of the bin into the washing machine with brusque movements. Then she was storming right back out of the room, and a few minutes later my shift ended, so it didn't matter anymore.

The laundry was only my first housekeeping duty of the day, but my second proved to be mercifully Trix-free. Michelle had ended up on the same music-room maintenance shift as I had, though. As I wiped the dust from a flute and then a French horn, she meandered closer with the clarinet she was polishing.

"It's stupid how they make us keep everything in here in perfect shape when no one ever uses the equipment, isn't it?" she murmured as if she was afraid of being overheard. Which, to be fair, was a legitimate concern in this place.

"What, you don't live for wiping down neglected musical instruments?" I said with a teasing arch of my eyebrows.

She giggled and gave the clarinet another swipe with her cloth. Even while she was complaining about the task, she was still making a thorough job of it. Why risk the potential wrath over something that small?

"I like the way you talk," she said, her elbow brushing

mine in an unmistakably deliberate motion. "You say what you think—what everyone is thinking, a lot of the time. You're not afraid to tell it like it is."

That statement in combination with the vast number of things she clearly didn't know about me left me choking on a guffaw. I managed to swallow my sputter of laughter.

"Yes," I said, with a dollop of irony that went right over her head. "I absolutely do."

"Do you want to hang out sometime later?"

She glanced at me sideways as she asked, a hint of her previous blush coming back. There wasn't a whole lot to do for fun at Roseborne College. An invite to hang out was basically an invite to seek out the spot where we were least likely to be interrupted and see how fast we could get each other off.

Why shouldn't I, if she was offering that blatantly? I'd enjoy myself at least a little, and she seemed to think she'd enjoy herself a lot, so I'd hardly be using her. No one here expected any encounter to turn into a real relationship.

But.

My thoughts slipped back to a recent and yet distant memory of my hands tracing warm skin, of a perfect little gasp of pleasure by my ear, of a smell like fresh clementines and nutmeg wiping away all traces of roses. Desire twanged through me that had nothing to do with the girl in front of me and snuffed out any interest I might have otherwise felt.

I wasn't sure I'd even be able to get it up with her. I'd only embarrass myself. So no, what would actually happen was neither of us would enjoy ourselves.

You had to know how to let people down easy. "Would you believe this just… isn't a good time?" I said in a meaningful way that left the meaning itself open to interpretation. She could fill in the blank with whatever she most wanted to believe. "Maybe another day."

"Sure," she said, blinking with sudden compassion based on whatever she'd imagined. "I'm sorry."

I waved off her unnecessary concern. "Think nothing of it."

The jangle of strummed strings brought both our heads up. We stared at the other student on music-room duty, a kid who didn't look a day over eighteen who'd turned up only a couple of months ago.

Apparently that hadn't been long enough for him to have learned the ropes. He'd tucked the banjo he'd been wiping down under his arm and, as we watched, strummed another chord. I cleared my throat in warning, even though it was almost definitely too late already.

None of us were allowed to play. I always left the area with the guitars to someone else to avoid any temptation. And here was this guy shifting his fingers over the frets with a goofy smile on his naïve face—

The smile snapped away an instant later as his entire expression stiffened. He wrenched his hand away from the strings, his fingers splaying rigidly. His thumb stuttered backward with a crack of bone. A cry burst out of him.

Professor Filch swept into the room a moment later to survey the room. He motioned briskly to the new guy. "It seems you forgot our policies about the instruments. Set it in its place, please, carefully. Excellent. Now come along and get that break set before it turns into something worse."

"Y-y-yes, sir," the guy stammered, and hurried after the professor when he turned on his heel, clutching his disfigured hand to his chest.

# CHAPTER FOUR

*Trix*

$\mathcal{I}$ might have been used to having to share a room with no privacy, but that didn't mean I liked it. In some ways, the dorms in Roseborne College were the worst accommodations I'd dealt with yet. The sheets were scratchy, and the night was punctuated by one girl's rattling snores and another's periodic whimpers. At least once an hour, someone sucked in a sharp breath that spoke of wordless pain.

I'd been relieved and kind of disbelieving when Dean Wainhouse had grudgingly agreed to let me stay on as long as I "pulled my weight." Now I was starting to wonder if my supposed enrollment at the college was more a way of teaching me a lesson about the dangers of getting what you asked for. Did he figure I'd come running to his office to say I'd changed my mind over a few days of discomfort? Not a chance.

Each of the dorm rooms had a tiny bathroom with a single toilet, but the four shower stalls that the nearly thirty of us girls had to share were located in a bathroom at the bottom of the stairs. After the first day I'd learned to be strategic. Since I wasn't sleeping all that well anyway, I got up while dawn was only just creeping through the window and took my turn under the water that sputtered between hot and cold no matter where I set the dial.

My third morning, I snuck down even earlier than the morning before. The dawn hadn't even started to glow on the horizon yet. I slipped through the dark past the bathroom and down the next flight of stairs to the main floor.

No one was stirring there either. I'd figured the staff would all still be asleep at this hour too. I went straight to the hall with the portraits and lifted Cade's off the wall.

This was the only object I'd found here that had any definite connection to him. Maybe it held more answers if I looked carefully enough.

I sat down on the floor and dug my fingers into the back of the frame. With several increasingly forceful tugs, I finally managed to detach the backing that held the painting in place. It came away in my hand.

I squinted at the rectangular piece in the dim light and then turned my attention to the frame and the back of the painting itself. Some part of me had been hoping for a message, a map, a diagram that would chart out the answers I needed. What I got was a whole lot of blank board and a little painted doodle near the top right corner.

A lump filled my throat as I peered closer at the casual sketch. It was a girl, captured in hasty strokes from head to waist, her wayward hair a vivid purple. Like mine had been dyed all those months ago when Cade had left. He'd doodled me.

Knowing that wasn't going to help me find him, but even if it was selfish, I couldn't help feeling a pang of relieved satisfaction that he'd been thinking of me even while we were so far apart.

The rest of the board was completely blank. I scanned it for a few minutes longer before fitting the pieces of the frame back together. As I turned it over, meaning to examine the main painting up close in case there was more to it than I'd deciphered before, a door squeaked across the way in the professors' hall.

My pulse hiccupped. I leapt to my feet, hung the painting in place as quickly as I could, and darted up the stairs. Better if none of them realized I understood that piece of art was connected to my brother.

I ducked into the bathroom, because I did still need my shower. By the time I got back upstairs, the other five girls in my room were just getting out of bed and dressing, just as I'd found them yesterday. They woke up a lot more slowly than I did.

I knew how to school my eyes away from other people's private business, but I'd still been unable to help noticing yesterday that the one girl's scars weren't limited to her face. They ran down her whole side, dappling and puckering her skin from shoulder to mid-calf and halfway down that arm. From the way she held herself as she pulled on her clothes, I had to wonder if she was the one who made those pained gasps in the night.

Shouldn't the college staff be doing something for her if she had injuries that weren't fully healed? Even painkillers to help get her through the night? But asking that would mean openly acknowledging that I'd noticed, and sating my curiosity wasn't worth the additional discomfort I'd probably cause her.

That morning, only three of us were left by the time she finished getting dressed. She stepped into her sneakers, and a breath hissed through her teeth so abruptly that my gaze jerked to her of its own accord.

She straightened herself up just as abruptly and walked out without a glance at me or the girl at the bed next to mine, although it was easy to see she was favoring her foot on her scarred side. Did her wounds extend that far and I just hadn't looked closely enough to notice? Christ, she had to be made of steel to keep up that stoic front.

My neighbor was perched on her bed, a compact open in one hand while she applied a sheen of lipstick with the other. It was the only make-up I'd seen her wear, making her mouth stand out like a third eye in her pale face. Her red hair, the shade my artificial orange only dreamed of being, fell softly around her face in its pageboy cut. She snapped the compact closed.

"Don't even try making nice with Violet," she said with a hint of a sneer, her glance toward the bed across from us making it clear she was talking about the scarred girl. "The stuff she did before she got here—she's a real degenerate. I know that much."

The girl—Violet?—looked more like someone had done awful things *to* her than the other way around. "What happened to her?" I had to ask.

Miss Lipstick shrugged. "Karma, presumably. It catches us all." Her lips twisted into a tight grin as if she'd made a joke she didn't find entirely funny herself.

I couldn't say I enjoyed her attitude, but this was one of the few times any of the students here had voluntarily spoken to me. Mostly they avoided me as if *I* were some kind of degenerate. Beggars couldn't be choosers.

"I'm Trix, by the way," I said, figuring any questions I wanted to ask would go over more smoothly if I offered a little politeness first.

"Delta," the other girl said in a bored tone. The tight grin remained. "Quite the school, isn't it?"

"It's definitely… interesting." I sank down on my own bed, creasing the blanket I'd tucked straight. "I don't suppose—you seem like you're pretty familiar with the place—do you remember a guy who started at the beginning of the school year named Cade?"

Delta let out a laugh that sounded more exasperated than anything else. "You never give up, do you? How many people have you asked that already?"

Her dismissive response brought my hackles up. My voice came out tart. "It's just a question. He's the whole reason I'm here at all, so yeah, I'm going to ask people about him." She must have overheard me questioning a few of our classmates—or maybe she'd seen Ryo when he'd been taking up my cause.

"Don't have a conniption," she said with an equally dismissive wave of her hand. "If I could tell you anything about him, I would. But I've got nothing."

Each time I got a non-answer like that, my frustration grew. Cade must have been here for long enough for *someone* to have paid attention. The proof was hanging in the hall downstairs. Even when I'd dragged a couple of students over to the painted portraits, neither of them had been able to tell me anything about who'd painted the one with Cade's symbol in the corner.

Even if he'd faded from everyone's minds like he had back home, the evidence wasn't completely gone. I just had to find more—something that would wake people up or point me in the right direction.

Something that would explain why this place was so strange and what part it had played in his disappearance.

In the meantime, to stay in the dean's good graces and get a better idea of exactly what Cade would have been through here, I had to keep up my "studies," if that was even the right word for the classes here. I tugged out the printed timetable that had been delivered to my bed on my first evening and looked it over. The college's approach to scheduling was as bizarre as just about everything else here. I was on a two-week rotation with some classes twice and others only once in that time, as well as my various maintenance duties.

For my third full day at Roseborne College, I was starting with my first stab at Composition class.

Delta had moved on from our conversation, pulling a notebook out of her bedside table and tucking it into her gaping yellow purse, but I might as well make as much use of her as I could.

"Hey," I said. "What should I expect from Composition?"

"Oh, are you heading there too?" She made a face, and I thought I saw a brief tremor quiver through her body. For the first time, I really considered her as a whole. The pallor of her skin didn't exactly look healthy. She was thinner than I'd noticed at a glance too. The tendons stood out in her neck, and her elbows jutted against her sleeves at sharp angles.

She shook herself, and any momentary weakness that had come over her fell away. "Come on, let's get breakfast before we deal with that. I've got Composition first thing too. You'll see what you're in for easier just going than me trying to tell you."

Wonderful. I gave the laces on my boots a quick tug to make sure they'd hold and followed her downstairs.

After a dreary breakfast of greasy scrambled eggs and dry toast, which Delta ate without a word, we headed to the class. The Composition classroom was the smallest I'd been in so far, but still nearly twice as big as our joint bedroom. Two rows of student desks stood in a semi-circle facing a lonely podium; the professor, who turned out to be the same woman who'd accused me of overstaying my welcome on my first day, sat at a larger desk off to the side near the door. According to my timetable, her name was Professor Hubert.

Several students were already in their seats, none of them anyone I'd exchanged more than a word or two with before. I sat at one end of the back row, near the windows and away from the teacher's desk, and Delta, to my surprise, opted to take the desk next to mine. I couldn't tell if that was an attempt at friendliness or her not bothering to pick a better spot.

After a couple more students trickled in, Professor Hubert got up from her desk and glided to the podium. When I'd first met her, I'd thought it was the lack of light that had given her an ashen quality. Now, under the harsh artificial illumination that compensated for the gloom beyond the windows, I realized she actually looked *more* wan in the brighter light, with a blueish-gray cast to her skin like ice over deep water. Her dark hair and large, equally dark eyes only made her pallor starker in contrast.

"All right, class," she said in the clipped, nasal voice I remembered. Nothing pale about that forceful tone. "Last time you were assigned a piece on shame. I expect we'll have time to get through them all." Her gaze rested on me for a moment. "Miss Corbyn, you're exempt this once due to missing the original assignment."

I nodded, with a rush of relief I wasn't prepared for—possibly prompted by nervous twitches and stiffened shoulders that had gripped my classmates when she'd first started speaking.

"Let's get started." The professor stepped back from the podium. "Mr. Taylor, why don't you start us off?"

The young man got up to make his way to the spot she'd just vacated. Within a matter of seconds after he started speaking, it became clear that the assignment hadn't been just "shame" but specifically "a time when you felt ashamed." Shifting his weight from one foot to another behind the podium, he related in a flat voice how one time when he was eight, he'd knocked an ice cream cone out of a younger kid's hand at a playground and how his parents had scolded him after.

When he finished, Professor Hubert, who was now propped against her desk, frowned. "I don't think you really went deep there, Mr. Taylor. The key to an effective composition is delving into the most meaningful moments you can offer. Cowardice doesn't do you any favors."

That was a not particularly academic analysis of his work. But the criticism appeared to hit the guy hard. He winced, his mouth drawing tight, and went to sit back down with his arm tucked around his belly as if he had a stomachache.

The girl Hubert called up next shot her a look I could only call defiant before launching into a story about a time she'd skipped volleyball practice to hang out with a guy she liked and almost—but not actually—been cut from the team. After the first run-through, I wasn't surprised to see the professor still frowning.

"Come on, people," she said after she'd sent the girl back to her seat with similar remarks, clapping her hands. "I need to see you're willing to put in the work here. We didn't bring you into this program so you could simply coast through it."

The girl who'd just read her piece hunched over her

desk, looking as pained as the first boy had. She aimed another glare at the professor.

Hubert either didn't notice or chose to ignore it. She turned to scan the room. "Miss Savas, what have you got for us?"

Delta stood up, her notebook clutched in both hands. She walked slowly but steadily up to the podium. Her lips parted with a shaky exhalation before she started to read.

"When I was in junior year, a new girl started at my school. Her father had transferred for work from another city. Right from her first day, she went around telling everyone she ran into how horribly allergic to shrimp she was. How we all had to be *so* careful not to poison her with it. As if a high school cafeteria is usually going to be serving seafood for lunch.

"The teachers all fawned over her and were constantly reassuring her that they'd watch out for her. She soaked up the attention so gleefully, I started thinking she probably wasn't allergic at all. She'd picked something easy to avoid and talked it up everywhere to get special consideration. As far as I could tell, it was pathetic, wanting everyone to be focused on her because of something like that instead of anything she'd actually done."

Delta drew herself straighter and dragged in a rough breath before continuing. The rest of us sat, frozen and silent, as she laid out the plan she'd made to "prove" that the new girl was faking, the stealth with which she'd sprinkled the crumbs of a crushed shrimp chip into the girl's soup one lunch hour—and the horrifying colors the girl's face had turned as her throat had closed up and her skin had broken out in massive hives.

"I could have killed her," Delta finished, her voice wavering. "If the ambulance had gotten there even a minute later, it might not have been in time. That's not what makes me most ashamed, though. What's really shameful is that I *didn't* regret it at the time. I told myself it was her own fault for flaunting her allergy in the first place. When I think back now to the way I thought then and the things I did because of it, it makes me feel sick. I want to shake myself, or slap my own face, but I'm not sure that would have made a difference."

The last words faded out. Her tense posture faltered, her shoulders curling slightly as she stared down at the page as if she was bracing for the lash of a whip. I couldn't help staring at her as the rawness of her confession and her current regret sank in.

I couldn't say it made me *like* her more, but there was obviously more going on beneath that haughty surface than I'd have guessed.

Professor Hubert pushed herself off her desk and gave a light round of applause. She was beaming, as if she saw Delta's wrenching story as something to celebrate.

"Now that's what I want you all to aspire to," she said, with an encouraging nod to my roommate. "Dig right to the heart of the matter and show us who you really are. Excellent, excellent. I hope our next speaker can follow Miss Savas up with similar honesty."

*That* was her goal with this class? To bully her students into admitting to the most horrible moments in their lives? A shiver ran through my body as I watched her pick her next target while Delta slipped back into place beside me.

Just when I thought this school couldn't get any more fucked up, it upped the ante. What the hell would the classes I hadn't attended yet hold?

# CHAPTER FIVE

*Elias*

Of course, Trix Corbyn would turn up in my class. Everyone ended up there eventually. I'd caught glimpses of her defiantly orange hair and her leather jacket in the halls over the past few days and heard disgruntled murmurs from some of the guys in the dorms. Now here she was, perched at her desk along with the eleven other students I wished I wasn't teaching.

At least she'd opted for a seat at the back, where I could let my gaze skim over her without it being obvious I wasn't letting myself so much as look at her.

The class was an hour of absurdity, stating it mildly. I knew that. All of the students in front of me knew that, except presumably Trix. Still, I'd had to go ahead and try to teach them today's math problem, and they'd had to go ahead and do their best to learn it, because if we didn't play our parts, the real staff of Roseborne College would crack the metaphorical whip.

The really sad thing, though, was that even after the years I'd spent here, as soon as I stepped in front of those watching faces, the urge to do this *right* gripped me. I had to prove I was up to the challenge, that I deserved the responsibility given. Elias DeLeon didn't back down.

Never mind that it was more a torture device than a responsibility, or that as far as I'd been able to tell, the challenge was impossible.

"Well," I said in my best professorial tone, managing not to glare at the traitorous numbers on the chalkboard beside me. "It seems we're working with power substitutions now. As some of you probably remember, we bring that strategy to bear when dealing with antiderivatives…"

The faces in front of me went tense with uneasy concentration as I lectured. Maybe they picked up a little of the theory even if they never really got to apply it? Not that I could take any pride in that fact when the knowledge wasn't going to do them any good anywhere else for the rest of their lives either.

Today's calculus equation was one of the more complex ones we'd tackled. I hadn't taken advanced mathematics on this scale before I'd come here, but I'd studied the textbook until I understood how it all came together. *No one else will put the work in for you if you don't,* my grandfather would have said. I'd managed that much. I just couldn't maintain whatever authority I'd taught myself while I had anyone else looking on.

Ryo Shibata leaned over to murmur something to Trix as I wrapped up my explanation. Part of me prickled at the disrespect, but that irritation rode on a wave of relief that he seemed to have redirected her from noticing the expected but eerie interference with our problem-solving.

"Who's willing to take a stab at this next stage?" I asked.

One of the guys in the front row offered. He gripped the piece of chalk I handed him determinedly and grimaced at the chalkboard's current display, and we continued on with our roles.

When the clock ticked over to ten to the hour, the problem was sprawled in a mess across the board, and we hadn't yet come up with the answer. "Better luck next time," I said, like I always did. The best part of the class was sweeping the brush over that board to wipe the whole headache away. Until tomorrow.

One class a day, five days a week, never quite enough time to shake off the pressure before it descended on me all over again. Maybe I wouldn't have minded as much if I'd still had more to do in between, but now that I'd worked through the initial hurdles, being allowed to attend regular classes where I could have achieved a goal or two would have been too welcome a distraction, no doubt. These days all I had were my assigned teachings, maintenance duties, and twice weekly "counseling" sessions.

Most of the students were already getting up, but Trix had simply sat up straighter in her seat, raising her hand. My chest tightened. When I pretended to be so occupied straightening the stack of textbooks on my desk that I hadn't noticed her, she got up, waving off whatever Ryo said to her, and strode toward me.

Hell, no. I'd promised myself no more investing in pointless causes. I didn't need any reminders of how epically I'd already failed in the areas that mattered most, no matter what other emotions her determined air stirred up inside me.

I grabbed one copy of the textbook to prep for tomorrow's lesson and ducked out of the room without so much as a glance her way.

Even with the heavy book tucked under my arm, my feet didn't stop walking until they'd carried me right out of the school. The clouds congealing in the sky glowered down at me. I resisted the momentary desire to give them the middle finger—*A DeLeon is never uncouth*, my grandfather's voice admonished me from the back of my head—and let myself wander all the way down to the main wall with its draping of thorny brambles.

I didn't have to follow it far before I reached the scattered trees at the edge of the denser forest that would hide me from anyone watching from the main school building. There, my pace slowed. I considered the blooms I passed, stopping and studying the ruddy petals. This one looked fresh and healthy enough. This one was wilting along the edges. And this one—the outer petals were already half shriveled, threads of brown rot seeping down to the base. It wasn't holding on much longer.

That was the way of things. Some beings thrived and

others wasted away. There was only so much potential to go around.

I could tell myself that over and over, like the mantra it'd been since my childhood, but I couldn't say I completely believed it anymore. This place had beaten the faith out of me. I couldn't even believe it'd been the right faith to base my life around in the first place.

Although that epiphany I couldn't credit to the school.

The book I was holding twitched against my arm. I held it out in front of me, and the cover swung open of its own accord. At this point, the sight of the pages flipping as if in a sharp but deliberate wind was familiar enough not to be disturbing. After a brief ruffling, the book settled open to page fifty-four. Behold, tomorrow's problem. At least, tomorrow's problem as this book felt like presenting it right now. Who knew how it might change once we got into it?

My body balked for just a second. Then I sighed and sat down on the patchy grass with my back against an oak's trunk. Why put off work you can get done right away? That was the lazy route, and DeLeons weren't slackers.

While everyone else in my room was settling in for the night, I roamed around the library and then the first floor rooms, doing my best to occupy myself and ignore the creeping fatigue that demanded rest.

I *had* to sleep, at least a little. No amount of self-discipline could remove that need. But if I held my eyes open for as long as humanly possible, the sleep I did get could be brief and intense, if not completely satisfying.

It was never going to be satisfying, no matter how long I lay in bed. If I couldn't maximize the benefits, the most practical strategy was to minimize the unpleasant bits.

As I came around the staircase toward the dean's office, my gaze caught on a flash of orange hair. I halted.

Trix was standing in the hall next to the stairs, studying one of the portraits as if searching for a deeper meaning within it. As I watched, she sucked her lower lip under her teeth, the uncertain gesture at odds with the resolve in her stance.

A pang shot through my chest. A dozen things I'd have liked to say, half of them contradicting each other, rose up to my throat. Rather than risk them coming out, I backed away to the sitting room and forced myself to sink into one of the armchairs.

After a few minutes, her footsteps creaked up the stairs. I waited another few and then ventured out again.

Maybe it was because of that brief sighting, or maybe I'd have made the gesture anyway, but I headed into the kitchen to see what pickings were left after the dinner shift. The napkin I spread on the counter easily held a pear that was probably mealy if the ones we'd eaten at lunch were anything to go by, a hard roll I sliced open and stuffed with an equally hard chunk of cheese, and a tin of sardines that might or might not appeal. Beggars couldn't be choosers, as Trix probably would have said. And we were all beggars in this equation, really.

I knotted the corners of the napkin and headed outside. The clouds had partly cleared for the night, filmy strands drifting between swaths of deeper darkness that glinted with stars. The half-moon cast a thin glow over the lawn, but I'd walked this route enough times, with or without a gift, that I didn't need it to make my way into the woods. Most nights, I ended up out here. The cooler air kept me awake that much longer.

Because I did come bearing gifts, I picked my way toward the deepest part of the forest rather than sticking to the easier paths closer to the wall. I wasn't sure exactly how large the campus grounds were, but I could walk for nearly an hour in this direction before hitting the far end. Tonight, it took about twenty minutes at a steady pace before another set of feet crunched over the twig-strewn ground.

I stopped and turned around. The guy I'd been expecting stalked between the trees, his hands dug deep in his pockets and his hair so rumpled I could tell it was messy even in the barest glimmer of light that penetrated the leaves overhead. I guessed at this point, the way he was living, he didn't see much point in bothering with a comb.

*As soon as you let appearances go, you might as well throw it all away,* my grandfather muttered through my memories.

*Shut up, Grandpa,* I replied silently. Words I'd never dared say to his face while I had the chance.

"Pickings were pretty slim, as usual," I said, holding out the napkin.

The other guy took it and let the corners fall open. "Looks like a fucking feast to me. I'm not going to complain." He looked up at me, his mouth slanting into a crooked smile. "Thanks. It's always nice getting a little variety."

He dug into the roll-and-cheese with a ripping sound that made me think about what he must eat out here the rest of the time. I guessed most of that time he wasn't in a state where he cared.

I couldn't have said exactly why I'd started making these periodic overtures. It'd just seemed like a natural thing to do when I was wandering the woods during these hours anyway. Maybe the impulse had been sparked by the memory of the guy in front of me springing to his feet in the middle of one of his first math classes under my watch and shouting, "This is *bullshit*." A potent punch of honesty and anger that I'd never dared to express myself, as much as I agreed with it.

Not so different from the attitudes I appreciated in Trix, which I guessed was fitting.

Everything at this school *was* bullshit, but it gave me a small sense of satisfaction that I could make it a little less shitty for this one person who'd been willing to say that out loud. Normally I'd have walked on and let him eat in peace. This once, with a thread of tension I couldn't explain thrumming through my chest, my legs stayed locked in place.

"She's just gotten here," I found myself saying. "She's still looking for you."

Cade's shoulders went rigid under his bomber jacket. The look he shot me over the remaining half of the roll had an accusing vibe. "I can't see her. It's better if she doesn't know."

*Better for her or for* you? I thought, but didn't say. Who was I to criticize someone else for avoiding Trix when I'd just spent all day doing the same?

But she wasn't here for *me* anyway. She was here for the guy in front of me, even if she didn't know exactly what lay at the end of that search.

"I can't tell her anyway," I said. The first rule of Roseborne College was you couldn't talk about what was actually happening at Roseborne College, whether you liked it or not. "I'm just saying. Maybe, if she had the full picture—"

"No," he snapped, almost a growl, as he cut me off. "Don't you dare try to tell me what she needs. I know her. You don't have a fucking clue." He looked down at the remaining food I'd brought him and then back up at me. His tone softened slightly. "Eventually they'll have to kick her out, or she'll give up. As long as no one gives her any reason to hope."

They weren't likely to at this point, but I didn't think Trix needed any outside party to supply her with hope. She seemed to generate plenty all on her own. The guy was right, though—I didn't really know her. Not anywhere near the way he did.

And that might have been why the defeat in his voice

rubbed me the wrong way. I managed to hold my tongue, just barely, at least from saying anything outright caustic.

"Well, you know where to find her if you ever change your mind," I said, and turned my back on him to ramble farther into the woods. The streaks of moonlight drifted like roaming specters with the shifting of the breeze through the leaves, but I welcomed their company. I'd take them over the ghosts waiting back by my bed any day.

# CHAPTER SIX

*Trix*

On my way up the staircase after lunch, I paused at the squeak of hinges in the righthand hall, the one Ryo had told me held only the professors' rooms. Peering over the railing, I saw a girl around my age slipping past a door just beyond the inner archway. Tear tracks marked her cheeks beneath her red-rimmed eyes, and her body trembled as she drew in a breath, apparently to get a hold of herself.

I eased back down the stairs. When I reached the hallway, a guy was ducking through the same doorway the girl had come out from, his mouth set in a flat line. The girl wasn't trembling anymore, but she swiped quickly at her eyes.

What fresh hell was going on over there? "Hey," I said. "Are you all right?"

The girl flinched at my voice and then glared at me. "I'm fine. Mind your own business."

Well, okay then. She stalked off, and I stepped closer to the door, wondering how much trouble I was likely to get in if I yanked it open to get a glimpse inside.

"There's no point in bothering," a sweetly clear voice said behind me. "It'll be locked. The counselor only lets one person in at a time."

I glanced over my shoulder to see Violet standing by the base of the stairs. After a few days, the fire-ravaged side of her face no longer sent a startled jolt through me, but I still had to contain the urge to ask if *she* was all right.

"Counselor?" I repeated, since she was apparently in a sharing mood. "Like, as in guidance?"

"Something like that. We have a session every week or so, mandatory. To work through our 'issues'." She made air quotes as she said the last word.

I hadn't made it through my first week yet, but I'd looked over my entire schedule pretty closely. I pulled it out and double-checked. "I don't have counseling on here anywhere, unless they call it something very different."

"Thank your lucky stars," Violet said in a singsong tone, and headed up the stairs without another word.

Great. Now I was even more confused—and even more curious. I eyed the door for a minute longer, but it seemed unlikely these sessions were super short. Maybe they only started up for students who'd been attending class for a certain length of time? I'd certainly seen plenty around here that could give a person "issues."

What if that room held the key to Cade's disappearance?

"What are you looking so serious about?" Ryo asked, ambling over to join me.

"I just found out about counseling, which I seem to be exempt from." I tipped my head toward the door. "I guess you must have those sessions too."

Ryo let out a short laugh. "It's nothing all that exciting. Blah blah blah, toxic this, meditate on that. I wouldn't feel left out."

He made it sound like no big deal. I'd have believed him if I hadn't seen how that girl had looked when she'd come out. Although maybe she just took the sessions more seriously than Ryo did? From what I'd seen, he cruised along without letting much of anything faze him, at least not in any overt way.

Which was part of the reason I still found it hard to take his friendliness completely at face value. Why was *he* so easygoing with me when my mere presence seemed to annoy just about everyone else? It couldn't be only that he saw me as a fellow interloper among the privileged set, because I'd seen quite a few other students since I'd stuck around who dressed casually or brashly enough for me to guess they had to be scholarship kids too, and they hadn't buddied up to me.

I didn't have to trust him to appreciate having a bit of company in this strange place, though. At least he seemed to try to answer my questions, even if he didn't have much of an answer to the most pressing ones.

And, being totally honest, he was very easy on the

eyes. A couple of times I'd found myself daydreaming about him coming to me with some information he'd stumbled on, and us joining forces as coconspirators to dig up all the secrets this place held. Shared glances across classrooms, huddling together as we spied on the professors from the shadows, a quick victory tumble into bed after we uncovered some thrilling revelation.

Those daydreams had been followed by a jab of guilt that I'd let my mind wander in that direction at all. I was here to find Cade, not to pick up guys. Obviously the coldness of the other students and the overall unsettling atmosphere were getting under my skin more than I'd have liked, that was all.

Who was I to think I deserved the enjoyment of even a quick hook-up, after all the blood on my hands?

"I guess I'm grasping at straws," I said. "I don't know what else to do." I just knew I had even less chance of picking up Cade's trail beyond the campus walls.

"Maybe you could use a break from all that searching and analyzing for clues," Ryo suggested in his offhand way. "Do you have anything in your schedule in the next hour or two? We could get out of here, take in some fresh air—I hear that's good for clearing your head."

It couldn't hurt, and he might open up more when we weren't surrounded by other students and the staff. I wasn't getting anywhere standing around in here. I swiveled on my heel. "Sure. You can give me the tour of the rest of campus now."

"I'll try to make it as entertaining as possible." He swept his arm toward the main door.

Outside, the clouds hung thick and heavy as they had the first day I'd arrived. I didn't think it'd rained in that time except a light shower I'd heard pattering against the bedroom window one night, but I couldn't remember the last time I'd seen the sun except filtered to a dull glow through that haze.

The breeze was heavy with dampness to match. I tugged my leather jacket closer around me, wishing I'd opted for my jeans and not the skirt and leggings that the chill seeped right through.

"Badminton court," Ryo said, gesturing to a span of cracked cement surrounded by a rusting chain-link fence. "As you can tell, not getting a lot of use these days. I think the forest over there is just for show—no one really goes in there. I guess you could call it atmospheric if you're into creepy."

"I'll pass on that." I scanned the lawn as we meandered around the side of the sprawling school building. "Are there any gardens or that sort of thing, other than the roses on the wall?"

Seeing all the vegetation around me made my fingers itch to add order to it and bring out more life and color. I'd always done my best thinking with a spade in my hand and the smell of fresh-turned earth filling my lungs. Plants didn't give a shit who you knew, whether you lived up to some random ideal, or how you were greasing the wheels for them. Give them the space and the sun they needed, and they'd unfurl without a single demand.

Ryo shook his head. "Not as far as I know. If there

were, they're probably lost to the weeds by now. I mean, the weeds got pretty much everything."

As we came around the back of the building, he pointed to a concrete rectangle in the ground up ahead, the gray tiles around the edges bordered by green tufts of those weeds. A metal stepladder was poised at one end. It wasn't until we walked closer that I realized it'd been the steps to a diving board, only with the board itself snapped off near the base. The broken pieces lay at the bottom of what had once been a swimming pool.

More weeds sprouted from the gaps in the walls. The only water the pool held was a few stagnant puddles on the grungy floor several feet below us. A mildewy stink wafted up, temporarily drowning out the rosy scent that permeated the campus.

"Must have been nice when this still got used," Ryo said. He sat down and let his legs dangle over the edge, then patted the tile next to him for me to join him. "That is, assuming it ever got warm enough that you'd want to jump in and cool off."

I hunkered down next to him, trying to picture the pool clean and filled with bright water, the sun beaming overhead. It must get warmer in the summer, right? But then, how many people would stick around for summer classes?

"I'm starting to think it's always gloomy here," I said, tipping my head back toward the gray sky. "That rosebush is going to get even more sparse if Mother Nature doesn't bring back the spring sun pretty soon."

Ryo's arm twitched as he moved to rub his mouth. I

glanced over at him just in time to see a shadow cross his face and disappear. Something I'd said had brought out the melancholy he mostly kept under wraps.

Seeing it gave me the courage to push more this time than I had before. "This school is pretty gloomy in general. And weird. Everyone takes the same classes? There don't seem to be any majors? And some of those classes— what the hell is up with Professor Hubert and Composition? Doesn't any of this seem incredibly strange to you?"

Ryo set his hands behind him and leaned back on them. "Sure, it's weird. You get used to it, though. Find the good parts and focus on them."

I couldn't hold back a guffaw. "*What* good parts?"

His gaze slid toward me, and a little smile curved his lips. "I'd say you're one of the good parts."

I hadn't expected the compliment. A tingle of heat raced up my neck and over my cheeks. I jerked my gaze away.

"I just got here. Anyway, this is a *college*. It's supposed to be preparing you for careers or whatever. I don't see how anything here manages that."

*And I'm pretty sure that somehow it's devouring at least the occasional student so thoroughly everyone who's ever met them forgets they even existed.*

Yeah, that still sounded just as crazy as it had four days ago. I rubbed my starburst scar instinctively.

"It's experimental," Ryo said. "A general grounding that's supposed to touch on every area we'd want touched. Believe me, no other college would have taken me, so it's not like I can complain that I should have picked a different option."

I looked at him again, raising my eyebrows. "You managed to get a scholarship to some exclusive experimental program, and you couldn't even have found a community college with a working swimming pool that would have given you a shot?"

Ryo looked right back at me. In that moment, the melancholy showed clearly behind his light brown eyes, as if the clouds above were being reflected from deep inside.

"How many other options did your brother have?" he asked quietly.

There'd been nothing accusing in his tone, but the question made me bristle before I could catch myself. "He could have gone all kinds of places if he'd wanted to," I said, the defensive words tumbling out faster than I could catch them. "He was really smart. He just didn't have a lot of patience for school."

Or much of anything else. I thought of the jobs he'd lost in the year after he'd graduated from high school—when we'd been meant to be saving for our own apartment to get away from the Monroes for good—and then shoved the memories aside. They felt too much like a betrayal.

"He came here because the scholarship people didn't seem to mind exactly what his grades were," I added. "They said they looked at how he'd performed in certain areas—I don't know." The truth was, even that part sounded absurd when I said it out loud. And then there were the parts I didn't want to say, that snagged in my throat with a piercing ache.

It hadn't just been what he'd thought he'd find here that had prompted his decision. He'd also been escaping what he'd been left with back home. He'd been escaping the horrible mess I'd made, without even knowing I was to blame.

So really, when you got down to it, this was all my fault.

"There you go," Ryo said, without letting on if he'd noticed any of my discomfort. "It was the same for me—not the best grades by a long shot, but they saw something there that told them I was the kind of candidate they were looking for." His smile twisted and then smoothed out. "Anyway, never mind about that. I shouldn't have brought him up. I know how frustrated you've got to be."

He picked up a couple of shards of the fiberglass that had made up the diving board, one of which had broken with a notch in the middle. With a few absent movements, he brushed the dirt off the slick surface and fit one piece into the other so they interlocked. Just like that, he'd produced a makeshift spinning top. He spun it on the concrete between us, and it whirled with a faint rasp.

The motion drew up a memory from ages ago: the old pocket watch my birth mother had treasured with its unusual tree-shaped etching on the gold case. The only thing of any value she'd held on to through all the scrambles for drug money. Hell, she'd cared more about that thing than me. As a preschooler, I'd dug it out of her boxes once and spun it from my hand, watching the light blink off it like the glints that caught on Ryo's creation.

When Mom had caught me, she'd clenched my hand so hard as she'd yelled at me that I hadn't been able to hold a crayon for a week.

Not what I wanted to be thinking about right now—or ever again. I'd left her and so much other awfulness behind, thanks to Cade.

I kicked the heels of my combat boots against the pool's crumbling interior with hollow-sounding thuds. "I just… Anything I do that isn't toward figuring out what happened to Cade, it feels like I'm letting him down."

"You're not," Ryo said. "I promise you you're not. How are you supposed to do all that figuring out if you never take the time to breathe and cut yourself a little slack?"

There was a rawness to those words under his gentle tone. The sense hit me that this was the first thing I'd heard him say totally honestly.

The fiberglass top wobbled to a stop. Ryo's hand shifted across the tiles toward mine and stopped a few inches away, as if he'd meant to take my hand but thought better of it at the last second. That was probably for the best. How could he really understand any of it?

"Let's pretend it's July," he said a moment later, leaning his weight back again. "Sun beaming down, sparkling off a full pool, the air so warm you can't wait to slip into the water. First thing I'd do is a cannonball. How about you?"

I couldn't stop the corner of my mouth from jumping upward. It was a nice thought—I'd give him that. I was about to play along just for a moment when a totally un-sunny sound split the air.

It sounded like a moan, stretched out low and

guttural, rising up from the forest across the lawn. Goose bumps rippled across my arms despite the protection of my jacket. My head jerked toward the trees, my legs freezing in place. "What the hell is that?"

Ryo's smile fell away completely. "Another good reason not to go wandering into the woods. We've got some interesting wildlife around here."

What, had that been a wolf's howl? I hadn't exactly encountered a wolf in the wild before, but the sound hadn't fit the movies I'd seen. Of course, movies lied.

The sound carried across campus a second time, louder than before. Nerves jittering, I pushed myself onto my feet. "I think I'll take that as my cue that I've had enough fresh air and it's time to get back to work."

# CHAPTER SEVEN

*Trix*

I came down to the second-floor landing for my second math class at Roseborne College and found Jenson Wynter staked out by the door with a small cluster of his fans. Oh, great.

The guy who'd started heckling me from the first moment I'd approached Roseborne College obviously wasn't an asshole to everyone. Whenever I saw him around school, he had at least a couple of other students with him, all grins and guffaws. In those moments when I saw him before he saw me, with his eyes lit up and his mouth curved with an easy grin of his own, I remembered my first impression of him: intriguingly good-looking.

But as soon as he did set eyes on me, the only intrigue in the air was why the hell he'd made it his personal mission to remind me I was here through atypical—and he seemed to think unworthy—

circumstances. I watched the transformation happen in front of me right now. His gaze caught on me, and it was like a cold wind passed over his expression, hardening every part of it.

"Haven't gotten your fill yet, huh?" he shot at me as I came over. "Having fun playing tourist while we work our asses off?"

His jabs were never all that specific, but somehow he managed to hit the right sensitive spots to make me wince inwardly. I *had* been watching everyone, engaging in classes only from something of a distance, knowing I was going to be out of here the second I'd gotten what I needed. When he put it that way, it seemed kind of slimy.

"I'm doing the work too," I said blandly, even though I'd gotten away with avoiding quite a bit of it so far. But what was the point in arguing with this guy about it?

Unfortunately, the way he was standing, I'd have to brush past him close enough to touch to get through the door to math class. I hesitated at the edge of his group of friends, looking pointedly at the classroom. A couple of the girls shifted out of the way with little smirks, but Jenson stayed where he was, the jerk.

He crossed his arms and tipped his head to one side innocently. "Oh, am I in your way? I didn't mean to interrupt your gawking." He stayed right where he was.

I glowered at him. I was about to push right past him, as little as I wanted to step that close, but at that moment the math teacher appeared in the doorway behind him.

"That's enough," he said to Jenson in an authoritative tone. "Move off to wherever you're supposed to be."

Jenson smiled at the other guy brightly, if a little brittlely. "Sure thing, teach."

That looked just great—having the teacher come to my rescue. Of course, he turned away and stalked back into the room the second Jenson eased to the side, not waiting for a thank you from me or even acknowledging my presence. Maybe that confrontation had been more about him disliking Jenson than caring what anyone said to me.

I took the same desk I had during my first math class, in the back corner, and studied the teacher as he wrote today's problem on the board. There was something kind of odd about the guy in general. He dressed professionally enough, his broad shoulders and buff chest perpetually covered though not completely disguised by a suit and tie, but unlike all the other staff I'd met here so far, he was young—no older than mid-twenties if I had to guess. His tan, strong-jawed face was smooth, not even a hint of stubble, let alone any wrinkles. No gray flecked his close-cropped, coffee-brown hair.

The other students didn't react to him the same way they did our other professors either. I wouldn't say anyone appeared to *enjoy* this class, but no one cringed when he looked their way. At the end of class, they didn't flee the room at the same speed I'd usually seen.

Also weird—he hadn't looked my way at all that I could remember. I wasn't even sure of his name, since he hadn't bothered to introduce himself or ask where the hell I'd come from. My schedule said *DeLeon*, but I hadn't heard anyone using that name in class. A couple of the other students had called him "Elias" without any "Professor" or even "Mr." in front of it, which was a hell of a lot more casual than the other professors accepted.

Well, what did I expect from him? It wasn't as if my arrival had to be exciting news to everyone on campus. He'd probably heard the basics from the other staff before I'd turned up in his class. I'd rather he ignored me than turned a spotlight on my presence.

Unlike Friday of my first week here, Ryo wasn't in my second-week Monday class. I didn't know the girl who'd ended up sitting at my left. When the teacher—Elias? Professor DeLeon?—announced what page we'd be working from, I flipped open the textbook that had been waiting on the desk. Jenson's accusation about playing spectator while the regular students got down to work was still pricking at me from the inside. I could put in an effort to participate, if only just to prove him wrong.

The problem on the page was the same as the one Elias had written on the board. I eyed it, taking in the form of the numbers and lines. Math didn't come super easily to me, but I'd hammered plenty of it into my brain during my last couple of years of high school. I hadn't been sure I'd even apply to college, but if I wanted a chance at some kind of botany program so I could get paid to commune with plants on a professional level, I needed my math and sciences covered.

When I'd staked out a table in the library, Cade had always found me there. He'd sit across from me with his legs stretched out, his ankle resting against mine, as he studied whatever schematics—cars, appliances, industrial equipment—he was poring over that day. He'd always had a knack for taking mechanical things apart and putting them back together, so he'd figured he might as well get paid for it. Which would have worked out fine if he'd managed not to get into so many arguments with his bosses and customers.

The teacher's voice broke through my memories. He was explaining something about the specific functions involved in this equation. I forced myself to follow the words, tying them in my head to the problem on the page. One comment he made included a term I didn't recognize. I hesitated and then raised my hand.

When I lifted my gaze a second later, Elias had turned away to scrawl something on the board. I waited, my skin creeping with each passing moment I kept my arm in the air like a flag for attention, and then decided it wasn't worth it and jerked it back down. I'd probably be able to figure out what was going on from the context.

At least, I should have been able to. The first few steps of the problem flowed out coherently enough with each student who came up to add their bit. By the third part, I felt confident enough to raise my hand to volunteer—take that, Jenson Jerkface—but Elias's gaze slipped right over me as if he didn't even see me. The same thing happened when I offered for the fourth step.

I lowered my hand after he called up a guy from the other side of the room, my skin creeping for a different reason now. His icing me out was starting to feel deliberate. He wasn't just avoiding acknowledging me when he didn't need to—he was making an active effort to ignore me. Why wouldn't he want to check what the new student could do?

Maybe, like Jenson, he'd decided that if I wasn't an officially verified student, there was no point in treating me like I belonged. A flicker of irritation seared the edges of my discomfort. Shouldn't the teachers be a little more professional than that?

The guy he'd called up paused when he reached the board, and the numbers there distracted me from my frustration. Wait, that wasn't the equation we'd started with, was it? I could have sworn there'd been something to the power of three…

I glanced at my textbook, but the figures there reflected the ones on the board. So much for paying attention. I rubbed my eyes as the guy started scraping his chalk across the dark surface.

But it wasn't just me. Elias considered the board and launched into another explanation of the process that I'd swear didn't line up with the instructions he'd walked us through to begin with. As if we were suddenly dealing with a different sort of problem than we'd been faced with previously.

He altered a couple of the numbers on the chalkboard with quick swipes of the brush and filled them in with different ones. There was nothing accusing or critical in his voice, nothing to indicate he thought the students who'd contributed had done anything wrong. I frowned, watching closely—and one of the functions blurred before my eyes. A nine became an eight. A new set of brackets formed around a fraction. What the hell?

This time I didn't hesitate—my hand shot into the air. Our teacher *had* to have seen that, right? He'd been staring right at it. Staring at the figures while they'd outright shifted as if they had a life of their own. A shiver ran down my back.

Elias turned back toward us and blindly rambled on with his lecture, his gaze never traveling all the way to me. I gritted my teeth. He couldn't just pretend everything was okay, no matter what he thought about me.

"Sir," I said, tired of waiting. "*Sir.*"

A few of my classmates glanced over. Elias's jaw tensed as he finally let his eyes rest on me. "Yes?" he said in a terse voice.

"The numbers on the board just *changed*," I said. Hell, everyone must have noticed by now.

He blinked at me, schooling his face into mild confusion that I didn't believe for a second. "I think your mind must have wandered. Or you might want to look into getting glasses. This is what we've got to work with." He motioned toward the board.

No one else said a peep. I sank back into my chair, resisting the urge to throw my textbook at his falsely oblivious head.

So what? One more piece of weirdness in an already incredibly strange place. But the fact that I'd actually been trying to follow along and been foiled by whatever the hell was going on in this class made this particular affront niggle deeper.

If it'd been a different professor, I'd have kept my mouth shut. It was obvious they didn't give a shit how any of us felt about the paces they put us through. But Elias wasn't quite like the others, even if he had some specific issue with me. He felt more present—more human. So when class let out, I hurried straight to the front of the class to insist he give me a real answer. I was tired of being left in the dark.

He must have seen me coming or suspected I'd make that move. I was only halfway down the aisle when I spotted his dark hair vanishing past the doorway.

Fuck that. I hustled over as quickly as I could amid the other students, but by the time I reached the halls outside, Elias had slipped out of view.

It wasn't important anyway, I told myself. What happened in a math class had nothing to do with finding Cade. But how could I know that for sure when nothing here made any sense?

The vibration of my phone against my chest woke me up in the darkened bedroom. Staying flat on the bed, I pulled the phone out from where I'd carefully tucked it inside my camisole pajama top and turned off the silent alarm. I glanced at the signal bars, but just like every other time I'd checked them, I was completely out of service range. At least the device's other functions still worked.

I sat up carefully and yawned. Three hours wasn't anywhere near enough sleep. In the darkness, my roommates were little more than vague lumps along the walls. A blanket rustled here; a rough murmur carried from over there.

Beyond the high window, the wavering moan I'd heard by the pool the other day split the air. My skin twitched at it, my senses snapping fully alert. A couple of the other girls turned over, but the sound didn't appear to have woken anyone up.

Good. I didn't want any questions about this specific nighttime quest.

I slipped out of the bedroom on my socked feet, pulling a sweater over my camisole as I went. A long time ago, I'd learned the trick of walking down the stairs along the edge of the wall to avoid creaks. I'd just reached the second floor by the girl's bathroom when a figure came into view over by the classrooms, striding through the shadows.

I froze, my pulse stuttering. My eyes had adjusted to the dimness enough for me to make out broad shoulders on a tall form topped with a bristling of short, thick hair.

Was that Elias the math teacher? My forehead furrowing, I risked easing a little farther down the side hall to get a better view.

He passed through a streak of faint moonlight on his way to the hall opposite me, and the glimpse I got of his chiseled face confirmed it. He walked on as if he were going exactly where he was supposed to be, up the stairs to the male students' bedrooms.

I waited for a few minutes after he'd vanished up there to be sure he wasn't going to march back down, escorting some guy who'd gotten into trouble. Elias didn't return.

Did he sleep up there with the students? I'd noticed he didn't totally fit in with the other professors, but I'd assumed he was still part of the staff with whatever benefits they got.

What had *he* been doing up this late?

When the coast appeared clear, I pushed those questions aside and got on with my own quest. I slunk across the landing past the classroom doors, down the main staircase with its sweeping grandeur, and into the thick shadows around the foyer.

Despite the sparse blooms on the wall-climbing bushes, the smell of roses still lingered in the air. It was always a little stronger down here than in the bedrooms, where I could forget it if I wasn't thinking about it. It tickled my nose as I crept to the door of the dean's office.

I stopped there and held still for a moment, listening to the sounds of the building. There was a faint creak like the walls settling. A gust of wind warbled past the front door. No sign that anyone other than me was up and awake.

I dug the coffee shop reward card that I'd decided to potentially sacrifice to this cause out of the pocket of my pajama pants. I hadn't taken a close look at the mechanisms on the dean's door when I'd arrived, but I'd had plenty of time to consider the other inner doors since I'd started attending classes. Like everything else in this place, the planes of wood and the locks built into them were old, verging on antique—nothing I couldn't tackle. I'd popped my first lock when I was only ten, to steal back a treasured figurine my fifth grade teacher had taken from me.

The card eased between the door and the frame easily enough. I wiggled it against the bolt until I liked what I felt, and then dragged at it while twisting the knob.

I hadn't lost my touch. The lock clicked over, and the door swung open at my nudge.

Just in case someone got up for a midnight snack and came by this way, I closed the door behind me. Turning on the main lights didn't seem wise, but I tapped on the flashlight function on my phone so I could actually see for this search.

If there were records of Cade's time at Roseborne College anywhere, they'd be in the dean's possession. Maybe he'd lied to me; maybe he'd forgotten they existed —either way, I'd track them down.

Unless they'd vanished like the relics of my brother's existence back home had, along with everyone's memories of him.

I didn't let myself dwell on that last possibility. My phone's light skimmed over the hearth and the seating area around it. Nothing there looked like it contained any storage. I walked along the walls, touching the paneling, just in case.

A couple of the bookshelves at the other end of the room had cabinet doors on their bottom halves. I opened those with a glimmer of hope and found nothing but more books. With a grimace, I pulled out a couple of volumes.

They were both bound in old, pungent leather, as were

many of the volumes on the shelves above. The others were covered in aged cloth. The pages I opened shone yellow with age. The copyrights showed they'd been printed in the 1920s or before, all of them more than ninety years old. I couldn't spot a single newer book on any of the shelves.

The dean was a collector, I guessed. His personal library covered a wide variety of subjects, from educational strategies to legal history to poetry, but there wasn't going to be any information about Cade in there.

That just left the desk. *Come on, come on*, I thought at it as I tugged open one drawer and another.

The first one I checked held only a small, black bottle and blank paper that looked nearly as old as the stuff in the books. I held the bottle up to the light and realized it was ink. Okay… When I unscrewed the lid and swirled it around, the stuff inside didn't move. It was totally dry. Time for the dean to switch to pens, obviously.

The contents of the other drawers included a box of cigars, a pair of wire-rimmed spectacles, a wool scarf that'd gotten tatty, and a leather notebook that gave me another spark of hope. That spark dimmed when I opened it to find page after page of a shorthand notation I couldn't decipher. From the fading of the ink, it looked like all this writing had been done well before Cade's time here anyway.

Surely the school didn't operate without student records of any kind? I still hadn't seen any computers that might have held digital files either. How did they even find out about people like Cade and Ryo to offer them scholarships? Maybe there was a separate room just for records in the building somewhere...

I was just shutting the last drawer on the desk when footsteps rasped against the floor outside. My heart lurched. I darted around the desk, meaning to wait by the door to listen for when the passerby had moved on, but they were coming straight to me. The knob turned.

There wasn't really anywhere to hide where I could count on going undiscovered, and it'd look a hell of a lot worse if I made it clear I knew I was doing something shady. I stepped closer to the sofa and bent over it just as the door opened.

I straightened up with a little jump as if startled. Dean Wainhouse peered at me and flicked on the light. "Miss Corbyn. What are you doing in here?"

"I'm so sorry," I said, channeling my nerves into awkwardness. I motioned toward the sitting area. "I couldn't find something I brought with me, and I got the idea I might have left it in here when I was first talking to you, so I came down to check... The door wasn't locked. I didn't want to bother anyone."

I couldn't tell from the dean's steady gaze whether he believed me or not. "I would prefer if you have inquiries regarding this room that you wait until proper office hours," he said. "Did you find your item?"

"No. I guess it's just lost."

"Let me know what it is, and I'll keep an eye out."

Oh. Er. "It was just a pen," I said, grasping for the first thing that popped into my head that I could conceivably have misplaced. "A pretty one with this silver vine pattern on it, kind of like my tattoo." I pulled my sleeve up high enough to show what I meant. "One of my friends gave it to me. If you do find it, that would be great!"

"I'll let you know if I do. You'd better get back to your bed now."

Those last words came out in a subtly commanding tone that didn't leave any room for argument. I gave a little laugh and hurried past him into the foyer with another mumbled apology.

It felt too risky to poke around anymore tonight now that he was up and knew I'd been roaming around too. I meant to at least scan the halls as I went up for a door I hadn't gone past yet that might hold those elusive records, but by the time I'd climbed the first couple of steps, a dull ache had formed behind the bridge of my nose. As I continued on, the headache spread behind my eyes and through my skull with a throbbing pressure.

The pain radiated sharper until I could hardly concentrate on setting one foot in front of the other. At the top of the staircase, I had to stop for a moment, clutching the second floor railing and squeezing my eyes shut, before I could even keep walking. When I stumbled into my bedroom, the headache was full-out blaring, drowning out any thought other than seeking relief.

I flopped down on my bed, and before I'd even pulled my sheet over me, my mind escaped into the blackness of sleep.

# CHAPTER EIGHT

*Ryo*

Jenson Wynter and I had never been anything like friends, but I hadn't realized he was a total asshat until this past week. My usual approach to student life was to keep my head low and my nose clean so I could drift along without drama, but whatever gods that existed hadn't blessed me with infinite patience. When I caught his voice carrying out of the first-floor sitting room in that snarky tone he only took on with one person, I stopped in my tracks and strode over to the doorway.

Sure enough, there he was dusting the side tables while Trix whisked her broom across the floor, her back to him and her shoulders tensed. Of course the powers that be would have stuck them on cleaning duty together. Roseborne's staff were by far the biggest asshats in the place.

"If you can't handle the reality," Jenson started up again, and I barged between them, turning to face him with a *Try me* look. He was a tall guy, nearly six inches on me I'd bet, but whip thin whereas I actually bothered to work out now and then. If he ever pissed me off enough that we had to come to blows, I'd put the money on me.

"Why don't you shut your mouth for once?" I said. "Or maybe forever, if you can't tell when your comments aren't wanted?"

Jenson's eyes narrowed at me, but his stance stiffened at the same time. "I can say whatever I want," he retorted. "Who asked for your opinion?"

"You did, by making such a production that anyone walking by can hear you." I motioned toward Trix. "She's here. She's going to stay as long as she feels like it. Work out your daddy issues some other way, all right?"

His jaw tightened. It was something of a low blow, derived from a piece he'd delivered in Composition class last year. I didn't generally rub that kind of stuff in. But if he was going to harass Trix every moment she existed in his presence, he deserved it.

"It's okay," Trix said in her unflappable way, chucking the results of her sweeping from the pan into a garbage can. "I can ignore him. He's not the first loser I've ever had shoot their mouth off at me."

"We've got enough crap to deal with around here without him adding to it."

"And I don't suppose it ever occurred to you that I'm trying to cut through the crap?" Jenson said in a barbed tone. If he was trying to get at something in particular, the point went straight over my head.

"You're doing a shitty job of it then," I replied, and turned my back on him too to focus on Trix. "Are you finished with your chores for this shift?"

"I think so. Just got to put the broom away."

"I'll keep you company."

We walked past Jenson to the hall without another glance his way. He muttered something under his breath that from his tone was probably obscene. Water off my back, dude. As if I cared what some slick and smirking white-boy ass thought about me.

He couldn't tell me anything worse than I already told myself on a regular basis.

"I really was okay," Trix said as we made for the housecleaning supply room. "He's irritating, but it's not like he's going to do any serious damage with all his hassling."

"So, more like a mosquito than a bear on the scale of creatures you'd rather not deal with?" I suggested.

The half-hearted joke won me Trix's rare laugh. She leaned the broom against the wall inside the closet. "Yeah, that's a reasonable assessment."

I wanted to ask what sort of presence she'd label me as in the range of possible animals—or whatever other metaphors she felt like using—but I wasn't going to go all needy on her. That wasn't the idea at all. Just take it easy, enjoy her company and make mine as enjoyable as possible in return, and welcome the fact that I got this extra brightness in my life after all. The real mystery was how I'd gotten lucky enough to end up with even this much.

Trix glanced across the hall as she shut the closet, and her smile fell. Her gaze lingered on the line of portraits on the opposite wall. She was thinking about her brother, no doubt—frustrated that she hadn't unraveled more of whatever she imagined that mystery to be.

A pang shot through my chest. She cared so much that she'd come all this way to try to help him, not even knowing what kind of a mess she might get herself into. I wasn't sure she ever realized how impressive that devotion was. Who in my life had I ever sacrificed half that much for?

It was better not to answer that question.

Better to distract her from those worries too. As much as I'd found I loved seeing how resolve could cast a steely glint across Trix's face, taking her from pretty to outright gorgeous in an instant, it was a dead end. I couldn't tell her that, and if I'd tried to I knew she'd have refused to give up anyway, so the least I could do was give her other, more pleasant things to occupy herself with.

I glanced farther down the hall, and inspiration lit. "Breakfast was worse than usual today, wasn't it?" I remarked. It *had* been an incredibly grainy attempt at oatmeal with only pebble-hard raisins to add a little sweetness.

The face Trix pulled told me how much she agreed. "I've had worse," she said. "But not by much."

I grinned. "Here, it's an hour or so before anyone goes

on lunch duty. Let's see if we can scrounge up something halfway tasty with the ingredients on hand."

She arched a skeptical eyebrow at me, but I'd caught her attention. She followed me over to the kitchen, where the boiled oatmeal smell still hung in the air alongside the ever-present rose perfume.

I wasn't sure exactly how the staff arranged our cooking supplies. A truck came by with a delivery every weekend, but I never saw the workers speak to anyone here. Even when I'd tried a, "Hey, man," to the guy who'd been hefting the boxes over to the kitchen, he'd walked right by me without a twitch of his eyes, like a freaking zombie. I guessed I should be glad they'd never tried to eat our brains.

The food they brought generally appeared to be picked with about as much care as the undead would have brought to the task. If an item could be stale, it would be. The leafy vegetables were always wilting, the fruits bruised or under-ripe. Anything that came in a can would be the cheapest possible brand, mostly ones I'd never even heard of, and the flavor reflected the quality.

But—most of the time—the goal wasn't to outright poison us, and our ruling asshats did have some sense of variety, so each delivery came with one or two gems that I'd probably only have considered baseline quality if it wasn't in comparison to the rest. There were packets of old but useable spices at the back of one of the pantry shelves. I didn't risk them when I was on official cooking duty, but just for me, I didn't mind experimenting.

"Let's see." I riffled through the pantry shelves and

settled on a loaf of white bread—definitely stale, but edible—and the packet of cinnamon. From the industrial-sized fridge, I retrieved a couple of spare eggs and a gnarled orange.

Trix watched with a mix of curiosity and amusement. "What are you going to do with all that?"

"Improvise," I said. "It's not going to be a feast, exactly, but better than most of what our classmates are going to feed us. Cut the orange into quarters for me?"

As she gamely hacked away at the fruit, I cracked the eggs and whipped them up with a fork, since whisks were not a thing this kitchen had ever heard of. I sprinkled in a little cinnamon and then squeezed whatever juice I could out of the orange quarters Trix had cut. The citrus scent rose up to push back the oatmeal awfulness.

That tang with its hint of cinnamon brought back the memories of my mother's pancakes. It'd been years since I'd gotten to eat one of those, but the flavor was fresh enough in my mind that my mouth watered in an instant.

This concoction wasn't going to come close to touching those, but I'd do my best with what I had.

"Oh!" Trix said when I got out a few slices of the bread. "French toast. I didn't know orange juice went in that."

"It can, if you like things that taste good," I told her with a smile.

The egg mixture soaked into the bread, I hoped solving the worst of the dryness and overriding the stale flavor. I stuck a blob of margarine on a frying pan and tossed the saturated slices on as soon as it'd melted. The sizzling sent a sharper waft of that mouth-watering scent into the air.

"So, you're a chef in your spare time?" Trix asked, leaning back against the counter.

I let myself admire the lean lines of her arms, which her sleeves bared to the elbows, and the sleek curves that filled out her wiry frame. "Not really. I don't even like cooking all that much. But I do like food. When I get desperate for something I'm not going to have to choke down…" I motioned to the frying pan.

"Well, I approve of that impulse." She leaned over to sniff the pan. "How do you know when they're done?"

"When they haven't started smoking yet," I said. "A mistake I'll admit I've made at least a few times. My *real* talent is finding the usefulness in discarded things."

I plucked up the pieces of orange peel to demonstrate. With a few cuts of the knife, a twist here and a wiggle there, I'd fit them together into a crafted flower as vibrant as Trix's hair. She accepted it, the corners of her lips quirking upward. "So, you're an artist."

"I'm not sure I'd go that far." Especially after I'd let any kind of practice slide those last few years in the world outside. It wasn't as if I got much chance to do anything but fiddle around a bit here at Roseborne. What I'd really loved out there was finding some old piece of furniture someone had set out in the trash—a side table or an ottoman or a little bookshelf—that I could drag home, sand down, and refinish into something Mom would exclaim over. At least, I'd loved that while I still had the capacity to care.

Willing away those thoughts of the past, I flipped the slices. Victory! The cooked side was a near-perfect golden brown. By the time I'd grabbed a couple of plates, the toast was ready to come off.

It wasn't the prettiest meal I'd ever seen served, dribbles of egg worming along the edges of the toast and the cinnamon dust clustered together in patches here and there, but fuck, even without syrup, it tasted a million times better than this morning's oatmeal. I might not have been able to fully appreciate the flavors seeping over my tongue, but they brought enough pleasure that the dullness inside me couldn't fully mute it. I gulped down my first slice in a matter of seconds and was licking my fingers before I'd even quite processed it was done.

The second one I dug into more slowly so I could savor the bites, dredging every bit of satisfaction I could through the numbness that attempted to siphon it away. The slice still disappeared down my throat way too quickly.

Trix polished off the last few bites of her serving with a happy sigh that sent a quiver of stifled anticipation straight to my groin. She looked at her plate as if feeling betrayed that it hadn't replenished itself. "Yeah, I needed that." Her light green eyes lifted to meet mine. "Thank you. You really didn't have to—you don't have to do *anything* for me, you know."

I waved her comment off. "If I had to, I probably wouldn't want to. But I don't and I do."

She gave me a searching look that penetrated down to my bones. I thought of all the things I could have told her now, all the things I couldn't, and all the reasons I wouldn't have wanted to do either anyway. But there was a part of me that still ached to take her hand and say, "Look, this is how it is."

She deserved that, but she deserved so much that I couldn't give her. What would I really be offering but pain for her and a little absolution for myself?

I kept my mouth shut.

"Why me?" she said. "Why any of this? You only just met me."

What was in it for me, she was really asking. That question I could answer almost completely honestly.

I sidled a little closer to her at the counter where we'd been eating, holding her gaze. "I like you. Does there need to be more to it than that? I knew I liked you the moment I saw you walk in here the other day. There aren't a whole lot of things I like in this place, so I figure I might as well make the most of what I do."

Her eyes darkened, and she ducked her head. Her voice came out quiet. "You wouldn't say that if you really knew me—everything about me."

What secret was she always holding back? I couldn't bring myself to care. Because this was true too:

"It can't be anything worse than what I know about myself. And no matter what it is, I also know you're stubborn and loyal, and you don't let anyone get in the way of doing what you believe is right, and I haven't met many people who can say that either. I'm not asking for your hand in marriage, Trix. I just want to be around you as long as you're getting something out of being around me, for however long you end up staying here."

I slipped my hand around hers, as easily as if I'd been doing it for years. Trix's fingers tightened against my knuckles. She wet her lips, her stance rigid, her gaze fixed on my face.

"Oh, fuck it," she said, and leaned in to kiss me.

Yes, thank all that was holy. I touched her cheek with my other hand, drawing her closer as I kissed her back, careful not to outright demand anything. Her mouth was soft and buttery-tangy from the French toast. The pleasure it stirred was as dampened as the enjoyment I'd taken from the meal, but as far as I was concerned, that was all the Heaven I ever needed.

# CHAPTER NINE

*Trix*

The box on my schedule simply said, *2A. Tolerance. Marsden.* It was the only "Tolerance" class on my two-week schedule, and I hadn't met Professor Marsden yet. What the hell were they going to teach us there? How to be kind and loving to one another?

Somehow I didn't think so, or else they'd been incredibly ineffectual at conveying that lesson to most of the students here so far.

The classroom was at the back of the second floor, one I hadn't been in before. As I walked over, a couple of the other professors came stealing up the stairs—Hubert and a man whose name I didn't recall who'd instructed us in seemingly random sketching techniques during my art class last week. Hubert glanced over at the art professor and brushed a sprinkling of pale gray dust she must have just noticed off her shoulder.

I knew that stuff. It ended up sprinkled on my clothes every time I went down to the basement for laundry duty.

Why would any of the professors have been mucking around in that dank space? I hadn't poked around in the basement much because it'd seemed to be all maintenance-related rooms, nothing really to do with the students, but apparently I should give it a closer look when I had the chance.

For the moment, I had to focus on discovering what "Tolerance" meant at Roseborne College. I walked into the classroom and wavered just past the threshold, re-evaluating my expectations.

The room wasn't set up like most with their rows of desks, or even like the art room with its larger tables shoved close together. This was a science lab. The high, black-topped tables with their little sinks and the stools poised behind them made that obvious, even if they were an older style than we'd had at my high school back home.

Why shouldn't we have some kind of science class? I guessed that would make for a well-rounded education. But this wasn't what I'd been picturing from the class name at all.

A few students were already perched on the stools. I took one at a free table, not sure whether there'd be enough of us that we'd need to share. Violet came in, glanced around, and picked the table next to mine, giving me her unburnt side in profile. Her expression was tight, but I didn't think I'd ever seen her relaxed, so I couldn't draw any conclusions from that.

"Hey," I said. She'd bothered to talk to me a little

before—maybe she would again. "What's this class about, anyway?"

Violet turned to look at me, revealing the ravage down the middle of her face. Under the classroom lights, it was even more obvious that some of the smaller patches remained raw red. They weren't just scars but not-yet-healed wounds.

"Just one more thing to trudge through," she said. "You'll get used to it."

At that moment, the professor swept in. She was a petite woman with a full skirt that rustled over the floor, her salt-and-pepper curls pulled back from her rounded face by two tortoiseshell clips. She bent down by the desk that stretched most of the front of the room, twice as long as any of ours, and set out a row of plastic trays on its glossy surface.

"Let's see how you all fare today," she said with a brightness that felt more sharp than warm. "Come up and collect your supplies. As always, we'll proceed by order of experience from least to most, so Miss Corbyn—" Her gaze found me from across the room. "You'll begin. Your instructions and observation sheet are on your tray." She tapped the one at the beginning of the row.

The other nine students got up as I did. I approached the front desk warily, but the contents of the trays didn't reveal a whole lot. Mine held just a vial of clear liquid and a packet of beige powder. Most of the others had multiple vials or packets, none of them labeled. I guessed we were doing some kind of experiment.

My sheet was marked with the class and my name, followed by a chart for me to note the date and any observations I made at each of the numbered stages. Today was number one, obviously, and my very brief instruction sheet was labeled with a corresponding 1.

*Mix the powder into the water. Swivel vigorously to mix (do not shake). Drink the entire contents and note any physical sensations that emerge after five minutes.*

I was supposed to *drink* this stuff? My body balked before I'd even sat back down at my table. I hadn't been counting on experimenting on *myself.* And what effects did Professor Marsden expect this mysterious powder to have on me?

"You may proceed, Miss Corbyn," the professor said pointedly.

I opened the cap on the vial and then the powder packet with deliberate care to give me time to consider while I went through the motions. A sniff of the powder didn't give me any concern—all I got was a faint salty whiff. It *could* have just been lightly colored, finely ground salt. Tolerance: a test of what unknowns we were willing to accept from the teachers rather than refusing?

If these were regimented steps like Marsden had indicated, then everyone else in this room had passed through this stage before with no obvious harm done. The guy at the table in front of mine was on the back side of his observation sheet, with the chart filled all the way to stage forty-seven. How bad could it be?

In a matter of seconds, the powder dissolved into the

water with my swirling of the vial. The water looked just as clear as before. I gave it another sniff and set my jaw. I'd drunk, smoked, and snorted stuff from uncertain sources plenty of times in the past. Was I really going to chicken out and let the jerks around me think I really was the "tourist" Jenson had claimed?

Without letting any more doubts creep in, I tossed back the mixture.

It wasn't a large gulp—all down in one swallow. The light salty flavor lingered in my mouth, noticeable but not unpleasant. Professor Marsden motioned to the clock beside the door. "Five minutes," she reminded me. "Mr. Frum, you may proceed."

A guy at the far end of the room who barely looked old enough to be in college poured the contents of one of his two vials into the other and then used a little wooden stick to stir in a white powder. He hesitated for a second and then threw it back like I had. From the grimace he made, its flavor had been worse than mine.

The next student got down to work. The minute hand on the clock was almost at my five-minute mark, and a faint tingling sensation spread through my stomach. Maybe that was just anticipation or a psychosomatic effect? The feeling sank a little deeper, morphing into mild queasiness, but nothing I couldn't have ignored if I hadn't been paying close attention to my bodily functions. I noted it down on the chart, since that was the only thing I had to report.

There. That hadn't been so bad.

The boy who'd gone after me still had his mouth set in a grimace. As my queasiness faded, nearly as quickly as it'd come on, he scratched at the back of his neck and then his arms. His concoction had made him itchy? This had to be the weirdest class yet. I still didn't get what the purpose was. To test how we tolerated various minor discomforts?

I hadn't been paying much attention to the order the other students were working in. A girl at the front of the class, who I thought had gone third, jerked her hand to her belly, her shoulders going rigid. She held herself stiffly in place while I watched. A flush crept over her skin. After a few minutes, whatever she'd experienced appeared to fade. Her posture started to relax. She grabbed her pen and started to write on her chart.

And then the boy next to her started to wheeze.

All of us turned to look except Violet, who was mixing her various ingredients at the moment. The guy's back shuddered with each wracking breath, which sounded as if the air was being dragged into his lungs through the thinnest and rustiest of grates. He wobbled on his stool, a bluish cast coming over his cheeks. My own lungs tightened in anxiety.

"Hold steady through it," Professor Marsden said in a perfectly calm voice. "The effect will only be temporary."

That didn't look like it was going to help the guy now. He swayed so far with one strangled gulp of air that he slipped right off his seat. He managed to land on his feet, staggering and then doubling over with even more desperate wheezes.

I was already half off my chair, torn between going along with everyone else's inaction and the concern that was gripping me, when the girl across from Violet knifed over and retched into her sink. Whatever she'd had for lunch came up with a sputter and a splatter. She sucked in a ragged breath, braced herself, and then sat back with a swipe of her hand across her mouth.

It was as if that one response set off a chain reaction. The boy in front of Violet lurched forward to hurl the contents of his own stomach into his sink, coughing and gagging and then spewing more with a horrible groan. He was still hunched over the sink when Violet followed suit, just barely yanking her hair back with one hand before she ejected a flood of vomit into her sink.

My own stomach churned at the noises filling the room and the sour stench congealing in the air. My gaze snapped to the professor, but she was watching all this with a dispassionate expression.

"Don't forget to record your observations as accurately as possible," she said over the choked sounds. "And keep an eye on the time so you can report how long the symptoms lasted."

Was she fucking serious? Violet shuddered and puked again. The boy who'd been wheezing had managed to climb back onto his stool, his breaths evening out, but the guy in front of me had just flung himself toward his sink, all but clawing at his mouth. He sprayed water from the faucet over his face and then gagged and spat, his whole body shaking as if in the grips of a seizure.

The horror of the scene around me clenched my

innards so tightly that it took me a moment to break through my shock. Then I was sliding off my stool and marching to the front of the room as fast as my feet would take me.

"What the hell is this?" I demanded, planting myself right in front of Professor Marsden. "Making us sick isn't a class. You can't do shit like this to people."

She considered me without any more hint of concern than she'd had for her other students. "We're teaching you your limitations and how to recognize the signs that you've reached them," she said smoothly, as if that explanation made the sickening chaos around me any better. "So many of you have gone through life never realizing the damage you could be doing."

What was that even supposed to mean? "Don't be ridiculous," I said. "You're torturing us."

"How much do you know about educational processes?" Marsden asked haughtily. "Back to your seat, Miss Corbyn. I've heard enough."

As if I was going to listen to anything she said after what she'd just done. I spun toward the door instead, rushing out and down the stairs, the sickly stink still lingering in my nose and the sounds echoing through my mind.

The thump of my pulse chased one other thought in circles through my mind. I couldn't just stand there and let this crap happen to people. Whatever hold the school had over them, whatever power the professors might be exerting, there were limits. I'd get out of here, I'd walk the roads until I reached a town or my phone got reception again, and then I was bringing the police out here to treat these jackasses like the psychos they were.

A headache like the one I'd gotten last night cracked through my skull as I burst out the front doors. The pain expanded through my head with each hurried step toward the gates. I gritted my teeth and pushed on.

Maybe it was a coincidence; maybe the school was doing it to me somehow—it didn't matter. I couldn't give in. I had to get away from this place and force the assholes who ran it to face what they deserved.

Ignoring the throbbing blaze behind my eyes as well as I could, I gripped the heavy latch on the gate and yanked it down. At least, I meant to yank it down. The metal lever jarred in my hands. I shoved at it again and then stared at it as intently as I could through the haze of pain.

No lock held the latch in place. Nothing should have prevented it from opening. It simply... refused to.

"No," I muttered. "No, *no*." I wrenched at the latch again, slamming my shoulder against the wrought-iron bars at the same time. The metal joints clattered, but the gate didn't budge. The impact shot up my neck and rattled a fresh burst of pain across my skull.

The headache was starting to mess with my balance. I stumbled backward and found myself tipping over onto my ass. My tailbone twinged as I hit the ground. My fingers dug into the cool grass beneath that gray, ever-clouded sky.

A girl had been walking along the wall. She stopped several feet from me. Her voice reached me as if from an ocean of agony away.

"There's no point. We come in, but we don't go out."

"No," I mumbled once more, my body swaying backward. As the back of my head hit the grass and my mind dimmed, one final thought rose up.

If no one ever left, then Cade had to still be here, somewhere, one way or another.

# CHAPTER TEN

*Trix*

I woke up in my bed in the dorms with a vague echo of the headache lingering at my temples. Otherwise, I felt pretty normal physically, but the second my mind slipped back to the events that had brought me to this spot, my stomach clenched up in a ball of horror.

I was literally stuck here in this psycho college that was becoming more like a literal torture chamber by the minute. So were all the other students, I had to assume. And my foster brother had gotten caught up in the whole crazy situation somehow or other...

If the things I'd seen were how they treated the students actually attending classes, how much worse off was Cade? Was he even still *alive*?

That question made my stomach twist even tighter. I sat up on the bed, swiping my rumpled hair back from my face.

The overhead light was on, the view outside the window dark. It must be evening if not total night now. I'd been out for a while.

Not so long that my roommates had come to bed, though. The only other person in the room was Violet, sitting cross-legged on top of her blanket with her back to me as she wrote in that notebook of hers.

"Hey," I said, and she turned, glancing down briefly to add one more note. "Are you okay?" I asked.

I meant after the ordeal in Tolerance class, but as soon as I'd said the words, they felt ridiculous. How could anyone be *okay* here?

She lifted one shoulder in a partial shrug. "Same old, same old." Her expression was a little less tight than I remembered it being before. Did she appreciate that I'd tried to stand up to Professor Marsden on everyone's behalf, or did she just pity me for my failure to get anywhere with that cause?

A cool draft trickled through the room. I shivered and reached for my leather jacket, slung on the corner of the bedframe. The worn material that by now was perfectly molded to my body always comforted me, like an extra layer of defensive skin, when I pulled it on.

I'd wondered before why the dean had let me stay on at the school, if maybe he'd meant to prove a point to me. After everything I'd seen, I was starting to think it was the other way around. The staff got off on tormenting the students however they could—and most of my classmates acted more irritated by me than anything else. Had Dean Wainhouse let me stick around just to add an extra layer to their discomfort, like I was nothing more than a new tool in the school's arsenal?

God, I hoped not.

"I like your tat," Violet ventured unexpectedly, nodding to the vine on my forearm just before it disappeared under the sleeve. "Do you have any others?"

I shook my head. "I was meaning to get more—but there were other things I was saving up for first." That apartment Cade and I had been going to share. A real college, if I'd decided it was worth going after all. I paused and then decided to take advantage of my roommate's new willingness to talk. "How long have you been here?"

Violet looked away, her lips slanting downward as if the question pained her. "A couple years," she said. "After a while, there didn't seem to be much point in keeping track."

And I was going to assume the school didn't offer winter holidays or summer break or any other chance for the students to slip away and never come back. Had the people Violet once knew forgotten her as utterly as everyone back home had lost their memories of Cade? They must have, right? If not, there'd be relatives and friends banging on the gate out of the same concern that had brought me here.

What was the point of all this torture for *anyone*, even the staff? Somehow I doubted they laid it out in clear detail for the students.

"How did you end up here?" I asked Violet instead.

"I got a scholarship invitation, like it sounds like your

brother did. Things weren't... so great, back home. I thought it'd be a chance to try being someone else or whatever." Her laugh came out bitter.

"Do you have any idea why *you*?"

Her gaze came back to me, steady and solemn. "It's not that hard to figure out. Everyone they brought in has to know, I think, at least after the first few months. You can't bury yourself that far in denial. I know you think the classes are horrible, but—they do bring a lot of things to light."

Ryo had said something about how nothing I'd done could be worse than his own past. I'd thought he was just trying to make me feel better, but maybe he really felt that way too.

"You can't *really* think there's any way you could deserve to be treated like this," I said.

"I don't know. Maybe you just can't think of all the things people are actually capable of." She studied me. "Roseborne didn't pick you. You picked it. I don't know what that means."

I knew I'd been capable of crimes it made me sick to remember. But I didn't want to lay those out for this girl any more than I could expect her to spill her guts to me. We were practically strangers.

Before I could think of the right thing to say next, Delta breezed into the room. At her arrival, Violet swiveled away from me. Remembering the way the other girl had described her to me—*a degenerate*—I couldn't blame her for retreating.

Delta didn't seem to notice. She nodded at me approvingly with a swing of her smooth hair. "Good. You're up." She held out a piece of paper to me. "You missed Literary Analysis. Professor Carmichael gave me your first assignment to pass on."

I stared at the paper incredulously as I took it from her. A sputter of laughter broke from my throat. "And they're still giving me homework."

"They don't really go for excuses to skip out on the work," Delta said. Her legs wobbled just for an instant before she sat down on her own bed. I noticed again how emaciated she looked—had her features gotten even sharper, her hands even more skeletal, since I'd first wondered about her health?

How many rounds of Tolerance had she gone through since she'd first "enrolled"?

"Why don't you just say no?" I had to ask, glancing at Violet to include her in the question. "Refuse to play along? If you don't give them what they want…" Maybe the people running this place would let them go? Without even finishing the sentence, the optimism turned sour in my mouth. I didn't really believe it could be that easy.

For good reason, apparently. Delta guffawed. "Right. I'd rather not deal with *those* consequences, thank you. You should have gotten a pretty good taste of what they're capable of by now."

Consequences. It clicked in my head the way it hadn't quite before—the piercing headaches, right after I'd snooped in the dean's office and then again when I'd defied the professor. I'd known they were connected but not necessarily a direct cause and effect.

If the school or the staff in it had the power to punish us that way, how much worse could things get if we kept up any sort of defiance? Vomiting a few times every two weeks might not seem so bad in comparison.

We shouldn't have to make that awful choice in the first place, though. There had to be a way out. I just needed to find it.

I didn't say that out loud. I'd learned enough to be wary of admitting to any resistance, even if it was blaring in my head.

"Yeah." I waved the assignment paper in the air. "I guess I should get started on this, then."

Delta eyed me as I got up, obviously not completely buying my shift in attitude. "Be careful," she said. "Anything you're thinking about, someone's already tried it —and realized trying wasn't worth it at all."

Well, the people here were about to find out that Trix Corbyn didn't give up that easily.

There were too many students—potential witnesses and even informers?—still wandering around in the halls for me to feel comfortable poking into the mystery any further at this exact moment. My stomach grumbled briefly about the dinner I'd missed, but I couldn't summon any enthusiasm about going down to the cafeteria to pick through whatever was left of what probably hadn't been an enjoyable meal even when it'd been fresh-cooked and hot. Instead, I headed to the library.

I hadn't done any work in there before, only explored

the expansive room over the weekend and determined it didn't have any clues I could decipher. As I stepped inside now, I unfolded the paper Delta had given me.

*Corbyn* was written at the top, followed by a book title and author name, neither of which I recognized. *Read chapter twelve and deliver a thematic analysis of at least five minutes next class. Be sure to touch on both plot and character significances that are apparent.*

I already didn't like this professor just from the way they wrote. If I had my way, I wouldn't be here in another two weeks when my next Literary Analysis class came around, but I might as well check out the reading and see if I could determine how it might be significant to the situation I'd found myself in. Everything the staff asked of us seemed to have some underlying agenda.

It took me a while just to find the damn book. The volumes on the shelves were arranged in alphabetical order by author last name but also grouped into categories that weren't obvious to me. I had to search through five different spans of Ls before I stumbled on it.

The fabric-coated cover felt gritty under my fingers. I slid the book out, double-checked the title, and looked around for somewhere to sit. Apparently the people who ran this school didn't think students should be doing their library reading in the actual library, because the only furnishings were the bookshelves themselves.

Down one aisle, I found a footstool to allow the shorter students to reach the higher shelves. I perched on that and flipped through the book to the requested chapter.

*It was not a meeting Dolores looked toward without apprehension,* the first sentence read on the yellowed page, *nor was it one she could dismiss without a great weight on her conscience. Heavy of heart, she trudged up the steps to her family's townhouse.*

Obviously an uplifting piece. I squared my shoulders and forged onward.

Dolores, who appeared to be the heroine of the story, sat down to dinner with her parents in a shabby room. She reflected on her childhood spent in that same room, with her mother barking orders at her and kicking her when she didn't understand the expected tasks, her father smacking her around when he came home drunk. In the current moment, her mother wheedled her for money and called her a disgrace of a daughter in much more elaborate and vulgar language when she said she had none to spare. Her father hurled his mug at her head and then slammed her face into the tabletop so hard she stumbled out of the apartment with a broken, bleeding nose.

That was the chapter. As I read it, a detached part of my brain made snarky commentary about how maudlin the scene was, how pathetic Dolores's willingness to spend any time with these people in the first place, and what an over-the-top attempt it was to tug on the readers' heartstrings. But at the same time, with each passing sentence, fragments from my own past stirred to the surface.

My birth mother, shoving me to the side into a hot radiator and not even glancing over at my shriek while she'd been intent on upending the apartment in search of that hit she was sure she still had. My first foster father, making me stand naked in front of him every morning before I got dressed so he could "inspect" me—never touching, but his eyes crawling over my skin like worms. My second foster mother, ramming my head into a sink of hot, soapy water and holding it there until I nearly blacked out, because she didn't think I was washing the dishes thoroughly enough. When I was four, then five, then eight.

I pushed the memories aside like I'd learned to do so long ago it'd become instinctive. The past was past. It couldn't hurt me now. I hoped those fuckers rotted in hell, and that was all the thought they were worth. But by the time I'd finished the chapter, more fragments were clamoring to the surface so quickly I couldn't fend them all off. Raised hands, harsh voices, shards of pain. More and more, until they drowned out the words on the page.

I dropped the book on the floor and stomped my foot on the cover as if the memories were coming from inside it, as if I could hold them back that way. My breath came out shaky. I hugged myself, blinking away flashes of images.

Think of the good things instead. Think of Cade's smile that first day when he'd welcomed me. Think of the "fort" we'd staked out as ours between the leaning maple and the old backyard shed. Think of the flowers I'd coaxed into blooming outside the Monroes' house. Think of—

Another girl's giggle rose up from the depths of my mind, severing those moments. The remembered sound set my teeth on edge in an instant. A flick of dyed black hair and a glimpse of kohl-lined eyes. A sniffle and a sob.

Fuck, no. I pressed my hands to my eyes so hard the heels dug in. The stinging right there in the present dulled the memories a little. I added the jiggling of my feet against the ground, the press of my teeth into my lip until a thread of blood seeped over my tongue.

When the barrage finally faded, I felt as wrung out as if I'd been running for my life. I picked up the book gingerly and marched it back to its spot. The uneasiness lingered even if the images weren't hitting me so forcefully now.

I had to do something else, something *now*, something real.

On my way to the library door, the electric lights snapped off. I froze in the sudden darkness. It took a moment for understanding to sink in. I must have been in the room for longer than I'd realized. At eleven o'clock each night, the lights in all the common areas shut off as if on a timer.

Perfect timing for *me* to get a little investigating in.

I slipped out into the hall and down to the first floor, but this time I walked right past the dean's office, as well as the row of paintings. I'd been meaning to figure out what Professor Hubert might have been up to in the basement earlier today. Maybe I'd find some bigger answers down there.

As I descended the steps into the cooler air, I used my phone for light. The concrete walls looked eerie in the thin glow. My shoes scraped the rough floor with each step.

The laundry room stood right at the base of the stairs. Beyond that I found a furnace room, a supply room full of old desks and chairs, and... the hall ended there.

I turned on my heel, frowning, searching the walls as if I might have missed an entire doorway on my first pass. This space couldn't have filled more than a third of the total area of the building. What kind of place only had a fraction of a basement?

A place that had a second section of basement that could only be accessed somewhere else?

I'd already explored this side of the first floor pretty thoroughly. A cursory check confirmed that there were no staircases or doors I'd missed. But then, if we were talking about a whole different side to the basement, its entrance would probably be on the other side of the building, right?

I'd only walked through the staff hallway once to check that it was all professors' offices—and, I supposed, their accommodations. It was possible I'd missed something there.

I slunk down that hallway, setting my feet carefully on the thick rug. The light from my phone glanced off the name plaques on the doors: Wainhouse, Marsden, Hubert, Carmichael, Filch, and a few others.

As the light passed over the door at the farthest end of the hall, I paused. In daylight, I'd taken the plaques to be pretty identical. The deeper shadows and the tone of the light brought out something different in that one. It had a tarnish to it the others didn't, and the edges of the letters were slightly worn down, as if the others had all been replaced more recently but no one had bothered with this one.

*Bushfell,* it said. I definitely hadn't heard anyone mention that name.

It could still be a professor whose class I wasn't scheduled for. Maybe the mysterious counselor? I could get in deep shit pushing farther. But how cautious could I afford to be when the teachers were literally poisoning us?

I leaned close to the door to listen for any sounds of activity on the other side. Then I fished the reward card I'd been carrying since last night out of my pocket and jammed it beside the door to jimmy the lock.

Thank the Lord for this aged building. The card did the trick on my first try. I eased the door open, ready to retreat the second I saw any sign that the room on the other side was occupied—

It wasn't a room. Beyond the doorway, a flight of stairs led down to a small landing.

My heart skipped a beat. I'd been right.

Breath sharp in my throat, I treaded down the concrete steps. The narrow walls closed around me. My phone's light quivered and seemed to dim slightly.

All that waited at the bottom of the steps in the pool of still, chilly air was another door. This one, my card didn't stand a chance against. The left side of the frame was bare, with the hinges presumably facing the other way, and the right side had a broad hasp-and-staple clasp with a heavy padlock holding it in place. From the patina on the lock, it'd been securing this entrance for a long time.

Who went to this much work to fortify a door that was already behind another locked—and disguised—door?

Someone who had something important beyond that entrance, something they *really* didn't want anyone discovering. But short of finding and stealing the key, I didn't see any way I'd ever get through to see what was on the other side.

*Elias*

Today's lunch offering was the kind of thing my grandfather would have dumped in the trash rather than even attempt to eat—but then, I could have said that for most of the dishes we were served at the college. Burnt spots blackened the edges of the grilled cheese sandwich, but somehow the cheese in the center wasn't melted. The banana I'd been served with it looked like it'd just come out of a fistfight—a fight it hadn't won.

But food was food, and I didn't have a gourmet chef I could turn to who'd whip up something better for me. I'd choked down a quarter of the alternately dry yet sticky sandwich when I noticed Trix making a beeline for my table. Her gaze was definitely fixed on me.

Shit. I should have been paying more attention. Thankfully, I'd picked a spot close to the door, like usual. It wasn't even that abnormal for me to scoop my lunch into a napkin and walk off to eat it elsewhere. The restless chatter of the cafeteria set my nerves on edge on the best of days.

Figuring that if she came after me, she'd be more likely to search inside the school than outside, I ducked out the front door. That turned out to be a bad call. Crossing the lawn, there was nowhere nearby to hustle to for cover when the door's hinges squeaked behind me several seconds later.

I had enough pride that I wasn't going to outright run away. I slowed my pace a little, accepting the inevitable, and took another grudging bite of my sandwich as if I'd simply wanted to take a stroll with my food for reasons that had nothing to do with the young woman striding over to me.

"Hey!" Trix's brashly clear voice rang out behind me. "Hey… Elias?"

I turned slowly, schooling my face into a quizzical expression. "That's my name."

She came to a stop in front of me, her arms crossed over her faded cotton blouse and her orange hair flicking at her cheeks with the breeze. "I wasn't totally sure what you wanted to go by, since I've been in your class twice, and you still haven't bothered to introduce yourself."

"Ah," I said neutrally. "I apologize for the oversight. If you just wanted to clarify, I prefer 'Elias,' but 'Mr. DeLeon' is also acceptable."

I moved as if to continue on my way, and Trix sidestepped to cut me off. "Okay. Elias. You want to explain why you've been dodging me like I've got some kind of plague you'll catch just by looking at me?"

My stomach sank, but I didn't let my discomfort show. *Never allow an opponent to see a weakness. No matter what you're feeling or how badly a deal is going, you put on a front of total confidence.*

"I'm not sure what you're talking about," I said.

She let out a derisive guffaw, which was about the response that answer deserved. "Oh, come on. You totally ignore me in class unless I'm practically screaming for you to acknowledge me. Every time I try to talk to you one-on-one, you vanish the second you see me coming. You just ran out of the cafeteria to get away from me."

"I didn't *run*," I felt the need to say. "And I take walks all the time. It has nothing to do with you."

"You just enjoy this gorgeous weather so much, do you?" She looked up at the clouded sky, her nose wrinkling.

The skepticism in her voice made my mouth twitch toward a smile for an instant before I caught it. She wore her defiance of authority so well, like she had from the moment she'd walked onto campus. As much as part of me enjoyed it, even wanted to revel in it, that attitude was dangerous too.

And it wasn't as if I could offer her anything useful in return.

"Was there something else you wanted to ask me about?" I said in my best teacher's voice, as if I had important business to attend to over in the woods I'd been walking toward and she was keeping me from it.

She frowned at me. "I just want to know why you're avoiding me. All the other professors are getting me involved in the lessons without any hesitation."

The words spilled out automatically. "I'm not a professor." As hopelessly frustrating as the damned math classes were, being associated with *them* was even worse.

"No?" Trix eyed me. "You stay in the student dorms, don't you? What *is* your deal, anyway?"

"I don't think that's really any of your business."

"But it's my business if you have some huge problem with me that means I can't keep up with class."

*No one can keep up with that class, not even me*, I wanted to say. *That's the whole point.* But the college came with rules, and one of those locked an explanation that blunt beneath my throat. I swallowed thickly.

This conversation had dragged out long enough. There *was* an honest answer I could give her, even if it wasn't as specific as she'd have liked.

"I don't have a problem with you," I said. "I just know that there's nothing I can do for you. I'm not going to pretend there is."

Trix kept studying me for a long moment. Then she exhaled roughly. "Of course there's nothing you can do for me," she said. "Because you can't even be bothered to find out what I've meant to talk to you about or what I might want. You can't because you won't try."

The remark stung deeper than I'd expected. "Beatrix, there really isn't—"

She jabbed a finger at me. "You know things I don't. You've got to have a better idea how things work here than just about anyone, even if you're not officially a professor. But all you care about is looking after yourself, I guess. Fine. I'll keep figuring things out on my own, and you can keep watching them torture us while you sit on your hands like they're tied."

She spun on her heel and stalked back toward the school with a swish of her skirt against her thighs. I watched her go, clutching my lunch and feeling more ineffectual than I ever had in my entire life. The damp air had turned the grilled cheese sandwich outright soggy while we'd talked.

I should have been subtler in my approach. I'd gone overboard with my avoidance, and that had tipped her off, and now she saw me as a fuck-up anyway. Next time— next time—

My fingers dug into the already battered banana. I didn't want to think about next time. I hardly wanted to think about *this* time. A hopeless sensation was creeping over me that there was no right answer, no way to win, no path to victory. Only more failure.

Staying where I was, I forced the rest of the sandwich down, tossed the banana toward the wall where it could eventually become fertilizer for the rosebush, and retraced my steps across the lawn at a slower pace. I'd have steered clear of the building for a while longer, except I was due for my first weekly counseling appointment, joy of all joys.

I approached the first-floor room with rising trepidation. You'd have thought my nightly torments would leave me numbed to the sorts of emotions the appointments were intended to provoke, but I was shit out of luck there. If anything, they set off a cyclical effect, the fresh visuals making the words stab harder, the lingering echoes of those encounters turning the nighttime voices more visceral. Another way this place reminded me that there was no winning here.

That maybe I'd never won at all, no matter what I'd done out in the "real" world.

At my scheduled time, I opened the door and stepped inside. The lock clicked over by some force of its own. As always, a plain chair stood in the middle of the small, white-walled room, but I never bothered to sit. It was easier to brace myself standing up.

Who would it be today? My sister? My grandmother? One of the many classmates and "friends" the school could twist to its use?

The rose scent flooded the room even stronger than if I'd been standing right in front of the blooms. The walls shimmered, and images appeared on them as if projected by an invisible device.

Trix's pale green eyes gazed at me from every direction. My body recoiled instinctively, but I had enough self-control not to try the door. I knew from plenty of experience that it never opened until the appointment was over.

The images of her were smiling at me, some close up on her face, some farther away so I could see her whole appealing figure. Somehow that smile was worse than the way she'd snapped at me less than an hour ago.

"Why the hell do you let them beat you down?" one

of her asked with a dismissive shake of her head. "They don't get to call the shots."

*But they do*, I answered silently. *In every goddamn way.*

"Were you ever even a kid?" another image teased. She loped toward the woods, waving for me to join her. "Come on. You've got a lot of making up for lost time to do. Let me guess—you've never even climbed a tree."

*Too many other more necessary things to do.* That's what my grandfather would have said. And God help me if I gave any indication I didn't appreciate all he was doing for us.

"Oh, fuck him," a third version of Trix said, as if she'd read my thoughts. Probably the powers that fueled this room could —probably that was why it'd presented me with her after the actual confrontation outside. "Just because someone helps you out doesn't mean they can't be an asshole. And that dude? From what you've told me, asshole through and through."

*You'd say the same thing about me if you'd been around me back then.*

More Trixes flitted past my view: Trix clambering out onto the school roof with the wind whipping her hair into a blaze of orange flame; Trix banging on a door with her teeth gritted tight. "Can't you talk to them or *something*? For fuck's sake, Elias." Trix tucked under a blanket that had fallen back with the rise and fall of her breath to show her bare shoulder, begging to be kissed. Trix staring up at me, her hair plastered to her head and her cheeks mud-flecked, her eyes watery with more than just the rain.

"What if it's not enough? We can't let them win. But I

feel like I'm doing everything I can, and it's just out of reach. What am I missing? *Please.*"

*I don't know. I don't have the answers. They're going to win, no matter what we do. They always win.*

A laugh spilled out of her as she whirled past me through a streak of moonlight, a moment of unfettered joy I knew was rare. A fantasy, all of it—none of these moments, good or bad, would ever really be mine. The invisible counselor was simply hammering that fact home, over and over, as if my heart hadn't already cracked apart in my chest.

Maybe, just this once, the forces around me had misjudged, though. I found myself sinking into the chair, surrounded by all these realities that weren't, thinking back to the reality that was—the accusation in her eyes and the demand in her voice on the lawn outside, the flicking of her hair in the wind. The potential balled in that lithely strong body.

I was never going to win. That hadn't changed. But there was a quieter message within the current that ran through the words that pelted me. It filled my heart with a sharper ache, but this once I let it in rather than pushing it away.

Trix didn't expect me to have all the answers. She didn't expect me to fix the world for her. She wasn't even sure she could do it herself, for all her bravado. All she'd asked of me, really, was that I try. Making the effort would matter to her so much more than the end result.

*I* was the one who cared about winning. Roseborne

College hadn't beaten the urge out of me yet. I'd almost let my old ways shackle me all over again.

She deserved better than that, even if the impending failure wrenched at me, even if I wanted to run away from it just like she'd accused me of. But I could do right by her, no matter how many people I'd let down before. I could be better than that.

I would be.

# CHAPTER TWELVE

*Trix*

Fourteen-year-old Cade's voice rolled over me from where he'd hunkered down on the bottom bunk next to me. He traced a finger along the inside of my arm. "We'd do anything for each other, wouldn't we, Baby Bea? Whatever you need, I'll be there for you. That goes both ways, right?"

There was something in his tone I'd never heard before, low and cajoling, but it sent a shiver through me like the glances I'd caught him giving me here and there over the last few months, as if he were measuring something in me with his eyes. The shiver tasted of both anticipation and uneasiness. Something was coming— something I might love or hate or maybe both at once.

"Of course," I said, because there was no other possible answer when it came to this boy. "Is something wrong?"

"I'm hoping nothing is." His breath grazed my ear. "I want you to prove it, so I know for sure."

The dream shifted; I turned over and found myself standing in the dark in a rain-slick alley, the Cade of five years later looming over a form that had fallen to the warped pavement. "You fucker!" he shouted as he kicked the guy in the gut, over and over. "You piece of fucking shit." When his legs started to wobble from the effort, he bent down and brought his fists into the pummeling.

I stood still and rigid, not wanting to watch, feeling I had to—*It's my fault; it was all my fault*—but the dream tipped me over and threw me out into the cramped space behind the garden shed that always smelled like turpentine. Cade's arms wrapped around my trembling shoulders as our foster father stomped around in the mudroom so loud his footsteps and furious voice carried right across the backyard.

Cade hugged me tighter. "Don't you worry, Trix. If he tries to touch you, he'll have to get through me first." With the unwavering confidence that somehow his eight-year-old self could take on a raging full-grown man.

"I don't want him to hurt you either," I choked out around a sob, clutching his arm, and he leaned his head close to mine, and we lurched forward into another memory, two years later, speeding down a steep, icy hill on a snow racer. The frigid wind wiped my hair from under my hat and bit into my cheeks. One of Cade's arms was still around me, his other extended to grip the handle.

We shot past a few trees and into view of a kids' plywood fort right in front of us. A shriek tore from my throat. Cade jerked on the handle, but it was too late. We slammed right into the boards, splinters flying as they snapped apart, and tumbled onto the snowy ground. Cade pulled me to him with a laugh bursting from his lungs, and as the panic washed away, I started laughing too—

—and then he was ripped away from me with a strangled sound, off into a black hole that wrenched his limbs from their sockets and tore his chest in half, blood and guts flying even as the monstrous mass swallowed him up. A cry broke from my lips. I hurled myself after him—

—and jolted upright on my bed in the Roseborne dorms, my forehead damp with sweat and my throat still stinging.

The impression of having watched my foster brother ripped apart lingered with a clenching of my stomach even as I took in the room, the sheets tangled around me, and my ragged breaths. For all I knew, something that horrible *had* happened to him here. Had I gotten even a little closer to understanding what? What had I actually accomplished in the week and a half I'd been here?

The gloom of the bedroom fed into those thoughts. I'd come up here after my afternoon cleaning duty to take a nap, half afraid I felt the prickling of another headache coming on, and it was still day outside, if muted by the constant clouds. The fractured sleep had only left my mind more muggy. I rubbed my temple.

"Everything all right?" Violet asked in that softly lilting voice that always surprised me. My head snapped around. She'd been perched on her bed so quietly that in my daze I hadn't noticed anyone was in the room.

It was the first time I could remember her expressing any actual concern for me, rather than grudgingly answering the occasional question. Maybe the concern I'd shown her yesterday had won me points I hadn't realized.

I hesitated, but the honest answer slipped out. "I feel like I'm not doing enough. I'm letting him down."

I could tell from the set of her mouth that I didn't need to spell out who I meant by "him." By now, everyone at the school must have heard or heard *of* my inquiries about Cade.

Violet's hands twisted in her lap. She looked down at them and then back at me. "I'm just saying, because you might not have noticed or bothered to look there, if you wanted to check out the whole school... There's a maintenance shed around the side."

The suggestion was vague, but her tone full of portent. Telling me something without outright telling me. I hoped even that wouldn't bring some punishment down on her.

I scrambled up with a skip of my pulse. "Thank you."

"Can't say it's definitely a favor," she muttered, but then, as I reached for the door, she added, "Trix?"

I looked back at her. "Yeah?"

"You know... You're here because you asked to stay. They weren't after you. If you tell them you're ready to leave, they might let you."

Her expression had tensed as she said the words. She was offering me a possible escape route that she knew was out of reach to every other student, including herself. My chest constricted.

Her idea did make sense. I'd insisted on staying—the staff had wanted me to leave. We'd struck a deal without any specific timeline. If I said I was done, that I'd walk away and forget this place the way they could probably compel me to do, would the gate open for me then?

Would I even want to?

"That's—that's a good point," I said. "I'll have to think about it."

Taking that way out would make Jenson happy, I supposed. He'd been rubbing in how little I belonged from the first moment I'd arrived. Maybe Elias would be overjoyed too, since he seemed to find my presence so off-putting. But frankly, I didn't give a shit what either of them thought.

The real question was whether I was actually helping anyone I cared about by staying here. What if Cade had been here and then gone, somehow or other, and I'd have found more answers out there? I might be wasting time focusing on this place when I only had a single shred of evidence he'd ever been here.

On my way down, I found Ryo leaning against the second-floor railing, waiting outside one of the classrooms. He smiled when he saw me—a slow, secretive smile that brought me back to the kitchen yesterday, to the press of his lips against mine and the toned muscle my exploring hands had discovered through his shirt.

He was a good kisser, giving and taking just the right amount to send a thrill through me from head to toe—a thrill that had become overwhelming as the minutes had slid by. He was too... nice to just drag into a corner somewhere and scratch an itch with. He'd be tender instead of rough, attentive instead of urgent, and that didn't work when nothing we did was supposed to mean anything.

But I did want to kiss him again. My gaze lingered on his lips for a moment, and a weird prickling of guilt washed over me.

I wasn't betraying anyone by fooling around with him. I didn't owe my chastity to anyone. As much as I might owe on my tab in other sorts of ways, any commitment like that had been severed more than a year ago, and not by me.

"Hey," I said, taking the route that would let me pass him. When I reached him, I tucked my hand around his for just a second and leaned in to steal a kiss as my way of giving that guilt the middle finger.

Ryo let out a pleased hum as he kissed me back. His smile was broader when we eased apart. "Now I'm twice as annoyed that I have to put up with Literary Analysis instead of running off somewhere with you."

What were the punishments around here for skipping class? I didn't think I wanted to encourage him to find out. I let go of him but brushed my fingers over his arm. "Maybe I'll find you later."

He chuckled. "I'll look forward to that."

What daylight there was had started to dwindle by the time I made it outside. The clouds had bruised with a purple hue. I wandered around the school and spotted the shed Violet had mentioned right away.

It wasn't even its own building, just a wooden

structure put together up against the brick side of the main school. The boards were scratched up and the shingles on the slanted roof curling. The door stood slightly ajar, which was probably why I'd only given it a brief glance before to confirm it held the sort of things I expected: rusting cans of paint, a tool kit, a rake, one of those old manual lawnmowers. Anything important wouldn't have been left that easily discovered.

Now, I pushed the door all the way open and stepped into the dim space. The door jarred against a cot set up behind it, the blankets rumpled and the mattress dipped in the middle.

I hadn't gone far enough in to notice that before, but even if I had, I doubted I'd have thought anything of it if Violet hadn't specifically nudged me toward this spot. I'd have assumed some lesser staff person who looked after the grounds slept out here. But then, I hadn't seen anyone working on the grounds since I'd arrived. From the layer of dust on the shelves opposite, no one had used those tools in a hell of a long time.

The bed was a little dusty too. It hadn't been slept in recently. I picked up the blanket to give it a quick shake, and sneezed at the particles that tickled into my nose. With my next breath, I froze.

Another scent had touched my senses: a tart, coppery smell that took me straight back to the last time I'd hugged Cade close.

It had already faded by the time I'd fully recognized it. Without thinking, I yanked the blanket to my nose. A deep inhale filled my lungs with that same scent—faint and with a hint of stale sweat, but unmistakable.

I had enough wherewithal to shove the door shut so no one walking by would see me and wonder what insanity had grabbed me. Then I knelt on the cot and bent down to press my nose to the thin pillow.

His smell lingered there too, like a ghost—present but so distant I couldn't quite grasp hold of it. Of him. A lump rose in my throat as I tipped my head to the side, soaking in that minor remnant of his existence.

How long ago had he last slept out here? The dust suggested it'd been at least a couple of months, but would a body's scent have clung on much longer than that? Had I missed finding him by a matter of weeks?

Why had he been sleeping out here instead of in the dorms?

My fingers curled into the rough sheet that covered the mattress. The impulse ran through my body to collect the linens and carry them back to my third-floor bed, to make some kind of a nest out of them, as if surrounding myself in these minor remnants of him would bring me closer to him in some concrete way.

I forced myself to let go and to climb off the cot. Then I searched through the rest of the shed, lifting every object that wasn't fixed in place, scouring the building from floor to ceiling, looking for any other sign Cade might have left behind.

There was nothing else that showed he'd ever been in here. Not even initials carved into the wood. And nothing to indicate where he might have gone next.

He hadn't slept here in months… so where was he sleeping now?

I ventured back outside into a brisk wind. The branches on the trees across the lawn rattled, their leaves whipping around. Layers of cloud scudded across the sky like currents in a broad river.

*Cade?* I thought, but his name stayed locked inside me. If he was close enough to hear me, wouldn't he be *here?* I'd come out onto the grounds in plain view often enough.

I circled the school building just to be sure there weren't any other structures nearby that I might not have given due attention to. The carriage house a short distance away on the other side of the building hadn't offered anything interesting when I'd looked through there before. Otherwise there was only the abandoned pool, the badminton court, and lots of grass and trees.

When I reached the shed again, I peered across the lawn with growing trepidation. There *could* be a cabin or something similar hidden away in the woods. Who knew what other secrets those trees might conceal?

I squared my shoulders and strode across the grass to the deeper shadows. My skin crawled as I passed between the first few trees. The leaves warbled with the wind, and I couldn't see much of anything except the vague silhouettes of the trunks. I doubted my phone's light would extend far enough to give me much comfort—it'd only turn the darkness beyond its range even more impenetrable.

Still, I might have kept going out of sheer

stubbornness if the shadows hadn't stirred other shapes from my memories. Not quite as fast as in the library yesterday but just as doggedly, scraps of the past washed through my mind. The form of one of my foster parents looming with a belt clutched in one hand. A figure standing beside my bed with his head bowed. The stuttering of light and darkness as car tires skidded out of control. The lumpy shapes in the high school janitor's closet vanishing into total blackness with the closing of the door.

The spray of shattered glass in a moonlit courtyard as a body fell.

My breath lurched ragged from my lungs, and in the back of my mind a gurgled exhalation echoed. I spun around, fumbling back toward the lawn. As soon as the last haze of sunlight fell across my face, the shadows inside me retreated too. I swiped my hands across my face as if I could shove the lingering traces of the past away that easily.

It was okay. I was fine. I'd come back tomorrow in the middle of the day when I could conduct a proper search, which made more sense anyway.

The queasiness that remained in my stomach only fueled my conviction. Everything in this place was toxic. The college or the staff who ran it or both had done something to my foster brother just like they were breaking down every other student here. Just like they were trying to break me.

I'd been through way too much before now to break

because of anything these pricks threw at me. I'd claw the truth out of them, I'd make my way to Cade, and until I had him by my side or knew how to put him there, I wasn't setting one foot outside those gates.

Maybe I didn't belong here, but they were stuck with me now.

# CHAPTER THIRTEEN

*Trix*

"I ... don't think you're going to like this class very much," Delta said in her offhand way as we headed to my very first encounter with Archery.

"Great. Now I'm really looking forward to it." I double-checked my timetable for the room number, even though the other girl should know where we were going. I'd have expected this subject to be an extension of gym class, but it wasn't being held in the fitness room. I guessed that small space was a little too cramped for shooting projectiles at targets across much of any range. Instead, we were assigned to one of the second-floor classrooms. "What am I in for now?"

"Just give it your best shot, and it'll probably be okay."

The note of uncertainty in her voice made my skin prickle, but the room we entered looked about as I would have pictured it. It was the biggest of the classrooms I'd encountered at Roseborne College so far, maybe twenty-five feet across and almost as wide, with a rack of bows against the wall near the door and five stations spread out across the floor in a row, each marked by a bin of arrows. Across from every station, a target that looked about as tall as I was stood at the far end of the room.

That all seemed pretty straightforward, but no doubt I'd discover there was some twist to this set-up.

Like so much of the furnishings and equipment at the school, the bows had an old-fashioned vibe: polished wood that was worn around the grip from decades of use, metal fixtures with a faint tarnish. I picked one up and found it substantial but not quite as heavy as I'd been prepared for. When I rested one of the ends on the ground, the other came up to my chin. The middle of the bow had a notch where it appeared the arrow rested to help one's aim.

Delta had already grabbed her bow and walked off to the farthest arrow station. I picked the station in the middle of the row at random. The arrows in the bin were wooden too, with feathered fletching at the back and a nock to fit the base against the string. The metal tip appeared to be a heck of a lot deadlier than anything you'd find on your average piece of sporting equipment. I tested the point warily with a finger and jerked my hand back at the pinch of pain.

Other than a dinky plastic set one of my early foster families had owned, which had barely moved its arrows more than a few feet and in seemingly random directions,

I'd never operated a bow before. Hopefully the professors didn't expect newcomers to be experts right off the bat.

The man I assumed was the Professor Roth listed on my timetable strode in a moment later. He had a houndish look that fit his class's subject matter, his jowls grayed with a hint of beard, his steel-gray hair hanging limp and floppy at either side of his dour face. He considered the few of us who'd already arrived with a slight nod toward me but no hint of friendliness. His round, dark eyes held a chill that touched me even at a distance.

More students were trickling in from behind him. He swept an arm toward them. "Come along, people, you know the drill. Pair up. Let's see…" He snapped his fingers toward a tall, slender figure who'd just ambled in. "Mr. Wynter, since you like to spend as much of your class time chatting as working on your skills, why don't you take our new arrival through the basics?"

Jenson's bright blue eyes came to rest on me, his mouth twisting into a smirk that seemed to mock both of us. Wonderful. Was it too late for me to dash over to join Delta instead? She hadn't offered to partner with me even though she must have known it'd be required, so I didn't figure she'd wanted the hassle, but she'd probably put up with me rather than make a scene out of it.

Of course, dealing with Jenson didn't have to be any kind of scene either. As he hefted a bow of his own and sauntered over to me, I found my initial apprehension faded quickly.

Who the hell was this guy, really, other than one more hopeless victim in this bizarre place, trying to make himself feel a little bigger by cutting me down a peg? Maybe he didn't like how I'd ended up here, but I *was* here now. I was going through everything the rest of them did. And he couldn't claim I wasn't committed when I'd decided I wasn't giving up on getting at least one person other than me free from Roseborne's torments.

Anything he said had way more to do with him than with me.

So, I stood my ground, gripping my bow and the arrow I'd picked up.

Jenson plucked an arrow of his own out of the bin. He cocked his head at me. "Still haven't gotten your fill of the horror show, huh?"

"Still haven't realized I've got bigger things to worry about than your opinion of me, huh?" I retorted. "It's a little sad that *you* don't have anything better to do than harass people who've never done anything to you."

"Let's not get into what I could say about someone whose life was so empty they decided to throw themselves into a godawful situation just for the hell of it."

"You obviously don't have a clue what it's like to care about another person enough that you'd go through anything for them."

Something flickered in his expression, a momentary tightening that might have been anger or pain or something else—I didn't have time to tell. My off-the-cuff remark had hit harder than I'd expected. Then, for some reason, it brought a slanted smile to his face, hard around the edges but still genuine enough that it reminded me of that first moment I'd seen him, before he'd opened his mouth, when I'd admired his looks.

"No," he said in an odd tone. "Obviously I don't." He motioned to the bow. "Are you going to shoot something with that thing or what?"

He was ready to get down to business now, was he? I raised the bow into the approximate position I thought I'd seen in movies. "Since I've never done this before, I think that's up to you as much as it is to me."

"Follow along, then." Rather than lifting his bow right away, he fit the arrow into place first, the wooden shaft against the hollow in the curved wood, the nock against the string. "Get your arrow ready before anything else. Make sure it's braced against the bow's rest to guide your aim."

I copied his movements, finding the arrow followed my intentions easily. Maybe I wouldn't need all that much help after all. "And then?"

"Bring the rest up to eye level," he said, demonstrating. "Sight along the arrow through the window above the rest. Pull back and release when you're sure you're pointing at what you want to hit."

Jenson positioned himself sideways, left foot forward, head turned toward the target. With an air of total confidence, he drew back the string, paused half a beat to adjust his aim, and let the arrow fly. It whipped through the air and dug into the target's second smallest ring with a thunk. He lowered the bow and dipped with a flourish of his free hand. "Remember that no applause is necessary."

I rolled my eyes. "I wasn't planning on offering any."

I set my feet the way he had and tested the string. It took some muscle to haul it back, taut as it was. Squinting along the arrow through the upper part of the hollow, I lined the point up with the red center of the target. Tensing my fingers, I stretched the string a little farther— and then let go.

The arrow flew forward with a twang, and smacked into the very edge of the target.

"Well," Jenson said with a little smirk, "at least you did hit the thing."

I didn't think I'd done *that* badly for my first try. "I was aiming at the center," I said, motioning with the bow. "Is there some other trick you didn't bother to tell me?"

"I figured with all those smarts you could figure it out yourself." He waved to the bow. "Look at the shape of the rest. Would you expect the arrow to fly perfectly straight? Take the veer into account. And resist the urge to put more power in after you've already lined things up. Get over-ambitious and risk throwing things off."

"Tips I could have used earlier," I muttered, and grabbed another arrow. "Okay. The arrow rest is on the right side, so I want to aim a little to the left to balance things out?"

"What did I say about smarts?" Jenson said in a voice that sounded more sarcastic than complimentary.

"Oh, shut up." I tugged back the string, tweaking my aim to compensate. The muscles in my shoulder twinged. Instinctively, I shifted to pull back farther—and Jenson touched my arm to stop me.

"Watch it," he said quietly. He was standing close

enough now that my skin tingled with the awareness of his presence. His fingers curved around my elbow so gently it was almost a caress. "Stay right here. Do you like what you see?"

I looked down the sight again and eased a smidge farther to the left. "I think so." I'd have liked *him* a lot better if he handled me with this much consideration the rest of the time.

"Then just let it go."

I opened my fingers. The arrow whipped through the air and struck the border between the second ring and the bullseye. Jenson stepped back with a low whistle. "Thanks all to my excellent teaching ability, clearly."

"Clearly," I said dryly, but the success had given my spirits a triumphant boost. This might be one class here I could actually enjoy. And something in his smile felt a little warmer now, or at least appreciative, as if I might have managed to knock a crack in the chilly attitude he'd had toward me. "What now? We take turns?"

"Why don't we make it five and five? Just clear your arrows when you've finished your shots."

He propped himself against the wall behind me to watch as I worked through my next three arrows. I made the same mistake of letting myself pull harder on the string at the last second, and that arrow flew right past the target to rap against the wall. The other two times, I took more care, and those hit the second ring. Next time I'd get the bullseye at least once, I told myself as I loped over to retrieve my arrows and Jenson's from his initial shot.

While he took his turn, I glanced around at our

classmates. They were operating under the same rule, five and then five, launching their arrows and switching positions with much more efficiency. Over at her station, Delta managed to land a bullseye. She let out a little cheer, but on her next shot, a wobble ran through her body. Her jaw clenched as she stiffened her stance in response, but the arrow scraped the floor a few feet in front of the target.

Jenson had just returned from reclaiming his arrows when Professor Roth clapped his hands. "You're all warmed up now. Time to up the ante. Partners, take your positions."

Jenson's expression tensed as he tossed the arrows into the bin. Without a word to me, he spun and stalked back toward the target. One person from each of the stations was doing the same thing. Walking over to the targets… and turning to stand right in front of them, their heads raised, their bodies rigid.

A chill squeezed around my gut. What kind of insanity was *this*?

"Five shots and then switch," Professor Roth was saying. "Take a point for each time you strike the target without hitting your partner; ten points each and you're done. I'd like to keep injuries to a minimum today, please."

He delivered that caution in a bored tone, as if seeing one of his students take an arrow to the arm or thigh—or, hell, chest—would be nothing more than a minor annoyance.

Jenson glowered at me where he'd braced himself in front of our target. He was tall enough that it only came up to his shoulders, and slim enough that plenty of surface area showed on either side of him, but that didn't mean he was safe. I hadn't even managed to hit the actual target every time during my first round of practice.

I remembered the sting when I'd pricked my finger on the arrow tip. Those things were sharp. One slip of the hand, and they could *kill* a person. Was everyone really going along with this?

It appeared they were. Delta's partner had already loosed one arrow toward her, striking the bottom right edge of the target a few inches from her calf. The guy next to me grimaced as he missed the target—but also, thankfully, his partner—entirely. No one looked *happy* about this turn to events, but no one had hesitated either.

*I don't think you're going to like this class very much*, Delta had said. Did they do this every time? A shiver ran down my back.

"Whenever you're ready, Miss Corbyn," the professor said pointedly.

My fingers clenched around the bow. I stared at Jenson, the only student in the college who'd been overtly hostile enough that I might have enjoyed the thought of taking a few shots at him—in my imagination. In reality, he was a living, breathing human being, and I was a total amateur. My hand was already trembling with nerves.

I'd hit him. It wasn't even a question. If I tried to aim at any part of the target, at least one time in those ten, I was going to fuck up and stab him open instead.

I looked over at Professor Roth. My body had already tensed automatically with the memory of the results of past defiance—the headaches, the blackouts. But the thought of going through with this made me balk even more.

"I'm not ready," I said. "I haven't had enough practice yet."

*I'm never going to have had enough practice to feel ready to do this.*

"I'm afraid that completing this task is part of the expectations of the class," Roth said, without a hint of regret. "All students are required to meet those expectations."

I swallowed hard. I'd never outright refused an assignment before. How much worse would I be making things for myself if I did? Would it jeopardize my deal to stay here—my chances of solving Cade's disappearance? If they kicked me out…

Resolve rose up through those doubts. If they kicked me out, I'd damn well find my way back in. I'd played along with everything they'd asked me to do so far. I'd drunk *poison* on command. This right here was my fucking line. For me, for Cade, and for every other student they were forcing into this sick game.

"No." I dropped the bow. It hit the floor with a thud that sounded thunderous. "I'm not shooting at a person. No one should have to do that. You can take your stupid 'classwork' and shove it up your—"

It wasn't like the headache. Agony lanced through my stomach so sudden and sharp I stumbled backward, clutching my belly as if it'd been slit open and I had to hold it together to keep my guts from spilling out.

Any words still in my throat seared away. I couldn't even cry out in pain. It gripped me too tightly, piercing even deeper all through my abdomen.

My legs gave, and I fell to my knees.

Professor Roth had leaned out the doorway. "Who's on infirmary duty?" he called into the hallway outside.

I gasped, and the sharp edges inside me seemed to grate together in an even more excruciating way. Two students hustled into the room. Roth pointed to me.

"Get her out of here. I expect she'll be unwell for quite some time."

Hands closed around my arms, the pressure lancing through my muscles. And then there wasn't anything left in my head but the agony.

# CHAPTER FOURTEEN

*Jenson*

"Wynter!"

The voice made my spine stiffen before I'd even looked around. Elias DeLeon was beckoning me from the doorway to the cafeteria with that authoritative attitude that raised all my hackles. He was hardly even a real teacher in his own class. He didn't get to order the rest of us around out here.

I *had* been going to head out the door anyway, as soon as I'd tossed the remains of my soggy cereal with its battered berries into the trash. I set the bowl on the dirty dishes table and ambled over with no intention of sticking around.

As I reached him, I spotted an unmistakable head of shaggy green-and-black hair lurking just behind his shoulder. Elias had roped Ryo into whatever he was up to as well? I tensed even more with an uneasy prickling that collected in my gut.

"What do you want, Eli?" I asked in an offhand tone, marking down a point for myself at the tightening of his jaw. It hadn't taken me long to figure out that he hated that nickname.

The irritation didn't sway him from his cause, though. "We need to talk," he said, with a tip of his head toward Ryo. "The three of us. We can use my classroom. Come on."

His demeanor still rubbed me the wrong way, but there was an urgency in his expression that I hadn't seen very often. And I didn't really want to get into a big argument about what this talk was probably about here in full view of most of our classmates.

"This had better be good," I said, but I walked with them up to the second floor.

Elias, being the anal, overachieving ass he was, had already set the textbooks for today's math class out on the desks. He propped himself against the teacher's desk as if he were about to lead that class for just the two of us. Ryo hopped up to sit on one of the desks, nudging the textbook behind him. I stayed by the door.

Elias folded his arms over his chest, making the muscles under that ever-present suit jacket bulge. Even clean-shaven, the hard lines of his face and the commanding air with which he held himself made it clear he was older than either of us—probably one of the oldest "students" here. I'd wondered idly in the past whether he'd simply come to the college late or been here a while. He'd already been a fixture here when I'd arrived a year and a half ago.

How much longer did he have? I didn't see any telltale signs of weakness, but he was the kind of guy who'd sooner off himself than let on that he was struggling.

"We need to discuss Beatrix," he said.

The detached way he said her full name made me want to punch him in the nose. As if he could claim to be any kind of authority on *her* while he was using the full name she made faces at. How much time had he even spent with her?

"Why are you calling me in for that?" I said, even though this was exactly what I'd expected. I hadn't promised to make this an *easy* talk.

He gave me what must have been his best "cut out the crap" look, which to be fair was pretty effective. "I have eyes. You might be getting off on heckling her right now, but that doesn't make you a disinterested party."

Oh, we were getting into the boardroom lingo now, were we? I leaned back against the wall with a roll of my eyes. "And you figure you're an 'interested' party?"

"Interested enough that I'm bothering to look out for her, which is more than you've attempted to do," Elias returned.

"So it doesn't count that I'm looking out for the fact that she shouldn't even *be* here, which you've got to know as much as I do?"

"Let's just hear what he has to say already, Jenson," Ryo broke in, as if he'd have put up any protest no matter how much of a prick anyone else was being rather than coasting along with the flow.

"Fine." Despite myself, I was kind of curious what the guy had to say. "Have the floor, teach."

Elias drew in a breath, looking as if he was feeling some regret about calling this huddle. "We're all… invested in her, to some extent. Can we agree on that?"

"Sure," Ryo said, and I shrugged, which was the easiest acknowledgment I could offer.

Elias nodded. "Do either of you *want* to see her putting herself through this hell anymore? Jenson is right about one thing—she doesn't belong here. As you've made abundantly clear to her in the most caustic possible way." His eyes narrowed on me for a moment.

"And making it caustically clear has worked so well," I said sarcastically. "Why don't you hassle the guy who's been doing the opposite of his bit?" I waved my hand toward Ryo, who as far as I could tell had been doing whatever he could to seduce Trix into staying.

"Of course I don't think she should be stuck here," Ryo said, his shoulders coming up defensively. "But she is —I think that's become incredibly obvious. Why shouldn't she have someone to turn to, someone who's at least willing to take the edge off instead of making the situation even more awful?"

"Oh, yeah, I'm sure you're only thinking about selfless generosity when you're getting cozy with her."

The remark came out more cutting than I'd expected, with a flare of irritation and, okay, maybe some jealousy that I'd never have admitted to him. I was *trying* to shove her out of here regardless of what satisfaction I might have gotten from her presence if I'd taken a different tactic, and this guy wanted to pretend making out with her was a heroic gesture.

Ryo snorted. "Says the dude who just admitted his campaign of harassment hasn't helped her one bit."

"I—"

"Shut up," Elias broke in. "We've all been stupid and self-centered about it—including me."

Huh. I wouldn't have expected Mr. Big Man on Campus to admit to any failing of his own. For that, I'd give the criticism he'd made of my strategy a temporary pass. "What are you talking about?"

Elias studied both of us in turn. "I think we've all been taking the approach that makes *us* the most comfortable and just told ourselves it's what's best for Beatrix too. But none of it is working. She's upset and confused, and now she's pushing back hard enough that she's getting herself hurt."

The memory of Trix crumpling in the archery room yesterday flashed through my mind with a jab of guilt. She hadn't even been protesting only on her own behalf—she'd been trying to defend all of us. Possibly me most of all, despite what a prick I'd been to her, since I was the one who'd have been directly in her line of fire if she'd gone through with Professor Roth's orders. She could talk shit back as well as I gave it to her and thumb her nose in the professors' faces, but she had a heart under all that swagger.

"If you're such an expert, what do you suggest we do differently?" I asked.

"I don't think she *is* stuck here," he said, focusing his pointed gaze on Ryo this time. "If we actually care what happens to her, we have to give her the best possible chance of getting out. Convince her that she isn't going to find what she's looking for here, that the best possible thing she can do for herself is leave us behind. And she has to believe we really are thinking about her and not just giving the idea lip service for brownie points or being a jerk for the hell of it."

That last bit was definitely directed at me.

I raised my eyebrows. "So, your big plan is that we *all* cozy up to her and then tell her to get the hell out of here?"

"Think of it however you want. We've all seen enough of her by now to have some idea how she'll react. Look at what you've been doing and be honest with yourself about whether you really think it's what's most likely to help *her*. I assume you're capable of that much?"

The barbed comment made me bristle all over again. Fuck this prick and his superiority complex. He'd ended up here just like we had—he didn't have any higher claim on human decency.

I pushed off the wall. "Isn't it more likely that you've realized that you screwed up, and now you're trying to make yourself feel better by spreading the blame around? Nice try, Glengarry Glen Ross. Watch me sort out my shit without you turning it into a new lesson plan."

Elias's jaw twitched, so I knew I'd struck a nerve

somewhere. "Jenson," he said, straightening up. "For once in your life—"

"You know fuckall about my life," I shot back before he could finish that sentence. The fact that I could say that at all made my stomach twist, and suddenly I was twice as angry. Fuck him, fuck Ryo, fuck this godforsaken college. "Take those intentions you think so highly of and ram them up your ass."

I shoved past the door and caught myself in the hall, closing my eyes. Anger was never a good emotion to show off uncontrolled. You had to reveal it wisely. I wasn't sure I'd been all that wise in there, but it definitely wouldn't do me any good to storm around the school where everyone else could see me.

With a few breaths, I'd gotten the turmoil inside me under control. Elias and his theories meant nothing. I could figure out my own way like I always had.

Neither he nor Ryo came out after me. Was Shibata actually buying into his bullshit? The guy really hadn't learned anything about the uselessness of chasing easy answers.

When I glanced around the main second-floor halls, my gaze immediately caught on the subject of our pathetic conversation-slash-lecture. Trix was standing across the way from me outside the library door. She was looking at a paper in her hand as if she needed to examine it closely before she made any further moves, but I could read the resistance in her stance. I'd balked the same way for probably the same reason enough times in the past.

Well, good if she was having second thoughts about this stand she'd decided to take. Maybe my approach would get me more traction now that yesterday's experience would have set her more off-balance. Elias didn't have a clue.

I walked over. "Literary Analysis assignment?" I asked. "Aren't those a bitch?"

Trix startled at the sound of my voice but steadied herself almost immediately. "Sounds like you don't enjoy them very much either," she said, eyeing me.

"The professors try their best, but it takes more than a little reading to faze me. And hey, it's what I signed up for. Do you think you're some kind of hero putting yourself through all this when you've got no business being here at all?"

"I think they made it my business when they did whatever they did to my brother," Trix muttered, turning away from me.

"Right, right. The grand quest. Did you make a whole lot of progress on that in the infirmary yesterday? I'm surprised to see you survived at all."

Her head whipped around again, her eyes flashing. Then she shook her head as if dismissing the momentary burst of emotion. Her tone came out dry rather than accusing. "Considering you're the one my arrows would have been skewering if I hadn't spoken up, you're the last person who should be hassling me about that."

"How do you know someone else didn't skewer me after you had to be dragged out of there?"

"Well, somehow I suspect that if someone had, you've

have led with that in this quest of *yours* to tell me how hopeless I am."

"I'm wounded by your assessment of me," I said, pressing my hand over my heart. "You should know I'm much more stoic than that."

"Only when you want to be, I'd bet," Trix retorted, and was that a hint of a smile playing with her lips?

A giddy jolt of emotion shot through me—that she could keep up with me so easily, that I'd gotten her caught up enough in the banter that she was starting to enjoy it— and then vanished under a cold surge of fear. I'd taken a step back before I'd even realized how my body was responding.

It wasn't *supposed* to be banter. She wasn't supposed to enjoy it—and neither was I. I knew what the end of that road looked like, and it wasn't pretty. It was a fucking mess that I never wanted to—

Trix knit her brow. "Are you all right?" she said, more puzzled than concerned, but that wasn't right either. Damn it.

"Don't start White Knight-ing me now too," I snapped out, fumbling for a halfway decent parting shot, and swiveled on my heel to saunter away as if I'd meant to end the conversation there all along.

I didn't look back the whole way up to the dorms. Coming into the empty bedroom, I stopped on the threshold and pressed my hand to my forehead.

Could I be honest with myself? Yes. The chill still congealing in my gut had so much more to do with me than it did Trix. Feeling that bit of warmth, the barest hint of comradery from her had terrified me—for my sake, not hers. It'd reminded me of how much I could gain and then have to lose all over again.

Fucking hell. I dropped down on my bed with a creak of the mattress and glared at the opposite wall.

Elias might not have been totally off-base after all. How much had I chosen my strategy based on what I really believed would urge Trix away and how much on what would give me the sturdiest shield to protect myself? Maybe I was acting like a stupid, selfish bastard. It wouldn't be the first time, not by far.

But after the groundwork I'd laid, what could I do that was better, that wouldn't crash into another epic mess? I had no idea.

# CHAPTER FIFTEEN

*Trix*

When I headed downstairs to breakfast, Delta was just a lump under her covers, but some of the other girls were still in the process of getting up too. It wasn't until I returned to grab a couple of things from my bedside table that I realized she'd never left her bed at all. A few locks of her red hair peeked from beneath the blanket, but that was all I could see of her.

I wavered on my feet, studying her, confirming from the rise and fall of the blanket that she was at least breathing. After the punishments I'd received for defying the professors, it was hard to assume that she was fine, just sleeping in. No one in our bedroom had ever stayed in bed past breakfast before. Even if she was okay *now*, she wouldn't stay okay if she ended up missing any classes or other duties she had scheduled.

She hadn't exactly been friendly to me, but she'd

helped me out a little here and there. If she got mad at me for waking her up, I could live with that.

I stepped over to the side of her bed. "Delta?" I said, quietly so I wouldn't startle her if she was already awake, just dozing.

Which apparently was the case. She mumbled something inarticulate and added a muffled, "What?"

"Are you all right? Do you need to go to the infirmary or anything?" I couldn't imagine anyone taking much comfort from the cold little room where I'd waited out the agony I'd been hit with during Archery, but maybe the young woman who'd appeared to check me over—and, I guessed, confirm I wasn't outright dying—would be more useful with a student who was sick due to natural causes rather than her own defiance.

"No. No, that's not going to do any good."

There was such a hopeless note in her voice that I couldn't quite bring myself to leave it at that. I groped for something else to say. "If you need me to let any of the professors know that you can't make it to class—"

"It's okay. They'll know." With a rustling of the sheet, she eased the covers down to her shoulders so she could peer up at me. "You go take care of your own stuff. Don't worry about me."

Seeing her made it even harder not to worry. I'd noticed her thinness before, but now her cheeks looked hollow, the form of her skull showing beneath her pale skin. Dark splotches glowered beneath her eyes. The fringe of hair along her forehead clung there as if she'd recently come out of a feverish sweat.

Just the motion of moving the covers seemed to have exhausted her. Her hand fell limp to her side. She barely managed to flick her fingers at me.

"It happens to the best of us," she added, her voice more thready by the moment. "I don't need pity."

The last comment stung, maybe more so because I also felt guilty for pushing her to talk in her frail state. I could take a hint—or really, this was more of a shove.

"All right. I hope you feel better after you get some more rest."

She pulled the covers back over her head, but not quickly enough to disguise a hoarse chuckle.

I didn't have a whole lot to do right away. I drifted downstairs and meandered through the halls. My explorations of the woods yesterday afternoon hadn't turned up anything informative. The secret to Cade's disappearance and the strange control the staff exerted over this school and its students still eluded me.

As I came around the base of the grand staircase with its poised suits of armor, a guy I vaguely recognized from a couple of my classes stumbled out of the room I'd been told was for counseling. He braced himself against the opposite wall for a few seconds, his posture shaky, before pushing himself onward down the hall. I glanced away as if I'd been minding my own business.

No other student had been waiting outside to take a turn. I lingered in the sitting room for several minutes, poking around at the furniture I'd recently cleaned and listening for footsteps, but it seemed this was a break between sessions.

That was one of the few rooms in the school I hadn't gotten any sort of look at yet. If I could even take a peek…

I strolled over and knocked lightly on the door, expecting a professor to answer. All I got was silence. I waited, my ears pricked for any sign of movement from the other side, and knocked again.

Nothing. Hmm. I hadn't heard a professor leaving the room either. Were they just ignoring me? I tried the doorknob gently and felt it catch against a lock.

I debated, glancing up and down the hall, and slipped my trusty reward card from my pocket. I'd have to palm it quickly, but I could easily give the same excuse I had with the dean's office—that the door had actually been unlocked. It wasn't likely anyone in there was paying enough attention to realize I'd already tested it.

In a furtive motion, I slid the card in by the frame and performed the same operation that had served me well on two doors here so far. Just like before, the lock disengaged, and the knob rotated in my grasp. I curled my fingers around the card to hide it and eased the door open, braced for a glare or a shout of dismay.

Neither came. The room on the other side was completely empty. It was easy to be sure of that because it held nothing at all except a single wooden chair in the middle of the space. The floor was the same dark hardwood as the rest of the building, the walls starkly white.

What the hell kind of "counseling" happened in here? And where had the counselor disappeared to?

I eased farther into the room and ran my fingers along the walls to confirm there wasn't some sort of hidden doorway. The only way in or out appeared to be the entrance I'd come through. I stood there for a couple of minutes, and then sank into the chair to see if that would provoke something.

The walls stared blankly back at me. Maybe "counseling" worked like some kind of sensory deprivation? If I sat here long enough, would the boredom of it all leave *me* shaking and crying?

I turned my head—and the wall beside me seemed to flash with the brightness of headlight beams. My pulse lurched automatically. When I looked at it straight on, it was just the same plain wall it'd been before. My mind was playing tricks.

More tricks than just that. As I scanned the room again, the impression of falling snow tickled the edges of my vision. Then the glint of broken glass. My muscles started to tense. Then—it must have come from the back of my head, but it sounded like it was coming from beyond these walls—the distant bark of a dog reached me.

Okay! Obviously whatever this room was normally used for, it was stirring up unfortunate associations for me. Or maybe those impressions were another sort of punishment for overstepping the school's boundaries. Either way, I'd had my fill. I sprang out of the chair and ducked out into the hall.

Outside, surrounded by the now-familiar dark wood paneling and the murmur of students' voices from around me and above, my nerves settled. My gaze slid down the hall past the professors' rooms to the door at the end. *Bushfell.* The one with its flight of stairs and the padlocked door at the bottom.

I should focus on that. It was the largest mystery I'd encountered in this place and the only one I hadn't been able to explore at all.

My fingers itched to fully distract myself from the unsettling flashes in the counseling room by riffling through the dean's office again, but I'd managed to get caught at that even in the middle of the night. He was probably in there during the day. And besides, I'd done a pretty thorough search the first time and not turned up any keys.

If he carried the one that opened that basement padlock, he must keep it on him. Or else in his private room? How much trouble would I get into if I managed to sneak in and poke around in there?

I didn't have time to find out right now. Checking my phone, I realized I'd ended up lingering in the counseling room for longer than it'd felt like. This week's Composition class was starting in five minutes.

I hustled up the stairs, looking around in case Delta might have recovered enough to emerge from the bedroom. I wasn't sure if she even had this Composition class with me too. It definitely didn't seem like it'd be good for her health to talk about some other horrible experience from her past. No doubt it was too much to hope that today we'd be writing about rainbows and kittens.

If Delta was supposed to be in the class, she didn't make an appearance. Professor Hubert made no remark on any absences as she surveyed the classroom from beneath her pile of brown hair. I inspected her clothes as surreptitiously as I could, checking for any hint of a key she might be carrying on a chain or in a pocket. Did the staff go down into their secret lair a lot?

Nothing revealed itself. Hubert rubbed her hands together and gave us a thin smile. "I wanted you to work on your next assignment with me here in class because many of the offerings last time left much to be desired. I don't want to see us become complacent. Let us plumb those depths! For today's theme, I'd like you to write about something that broke, whether through your actions or someone else's."

Glass shattering. Shards slicing through flesh to provoke that horrible wet gasp. My pulse stuttered, and my fingers clenched hard around my pen.

No way was I writing about that. She wanted something painful? Well, I'd watched a hell of a lot of things get broken over the years. I just had to narrow it down to something else.

My mind slipped back through time to the hand-me-down Barbie doll I'd treasured when I was six, even though her previous owner had chopped her hair close to the scalp and doodled all over her legs with permanent marker. It'd been the only toy that was actually *mine* back then.

I'd been playing with her in the living room when my foster mother had yelled at me to come help her cook dinner right that second, and I'd returned to my foster father's reddened face as he stomped his foot down on the doll.

*We don't leave our things lying around on the floor—or we lose those things.* Crunch. Snap. Face bashed in. Limbs snapped in half. Yeah, I had some depths to plumb there without touching on anything still raw.

I dove into those depths with the determination to milk the event for every drop of angst I could. I'd made it through a page of my school-issued notebook when Professor Hubert came up beside my desk.

"May I look over what you've got so far, Miss Corbyn?" she asked in a way that wasn't a question but an order.

I handed the notebook over and spun my pen between my fingers while she read. Maybe she'd think it was inconsequential because the broken thing had been a toy, even though I'd emphasized how meaningful it'd been to me to set up the horror that came after. Hopefully she'd give me a little slack on my first time going through this process.

The professor set the notebook on my desk with a humming sound I couldn't decipher. "You have a solid grasp on dramatics," she said. "But I can't help feeling there's a larger story you're avoiding here."

A shiver ran through my chest. "That's the whole story that has anything to do with the toy getting broken," I said.

Hubert gazed down at me steadily with her piercing eyes. "No," she said. "I mean there are other broken things that still have their hold on you, Miss Corbyn. We'll uncover them as we go."

She moved on to the next desk, leaving her words hanging in the air like a promise and a threat wrapped into one.

*Ryo*

Trix frowned at the row of windows along the north side of the school. She bobbed up on her toes to peer through one, but she didn't look any happier about it than before.

"It's too dim to make out much," she said, dropping back down and sweeping her orange waves back from her face. "And it doesn't look like there's any way to get in through those, short of breaking the panes—at least from the outside. Do you know if the windows open at all? Do the professors air their rooms out in the summer, even?"

"I can't remember," I said, which was true but also only a portion of the truth. After my first few months here at Roseborne College, I'd started to realize that the season never really changed. It was always this damp, gloomy New England mid-spring. I couldn't say I missed the snowy Pittsburgh winters a whole lot, but every now and then I still got a pang of homesickness for those bright summer days when the sun baked you where you stood.

There were certain comments that just wouldn't come out, though, even if I'd thought it was a good idea to say them. They could form in my head, but there was a barricade somewhere between my brain and my throat, let alone my tongue. We weren't allowed to explain or discuss what we'd determined about the college's workings with any specifics, even with other long-time students. This place liked to leave us in the dark in more ways than one. The newbies eventually figured out the basics for themselves.

"I don't think trying to sneak into their space would be the best idea anyway," I added, hoping I didn't need to say more than that. Trix had faced the staff's punishments already. And they had an uncanny ability to know when certain boundaries were crossed, at least within the school building. Out here in the open air, I felt safer—but only a little.

"I know." Trix's hands clenched as if she'd have liked to give the brick wall a punch or two to express her frustration. Instead, she let out the emotion with a rough sigh and turned to face me. "Have you ever noticed the dean or any of the professors carrying a key? On its own, or a whole ring of them, or whatever?"

I raised my eyebrows. "They're not going to be keen on you going in with a stolen key either."

"I'm not thinking about the offices. There's—" She cut herself off with a wary glance toward the building that told me she'd also learned to be cautious of how much the staff might perceive even when they weren't present. "There's something else I'd like to check out. I think it must be particularly important to them. Of course, who knows in this crazy place?"

"It's definitely got no shortage of secrets. But no, I haven't noticed any special keys." I wasn't sure what the "something else" she was talking about could be, but chances were it would get her into more trouble rather than less. I hadn't even been completely convinced by Elias's certainty that Trix could get free of Roseborne if she tried. The chances of her beating the staff at their own game seemed a thousand times less likely.

But of course that didn't stop her from giving it her all. This girl had nothing if not an iron will.

Case in point: At my remark, her mind had already leapt to another mystery she'd clearly been stewing over. She tapped my chest. "You said you have counseling sessions, right? I went into the room this morning—it was pretty barren. What, do you just sit in that chair and one of the professors talks at you?"

"Something like that." My gut tightened. If the room's effects were a conversation, then mine in there were always disorientingly fraught. I tried not to think about it at all when I didn't have to.

"Which professor handles the counseling? I didn't see any of them going in or out."

I wasn't sure how much I could manage to say about that. "I'm not sure," I said tentatively. "The way the sessions are set up, we don't really see them while it's happening. It might be more than one of them handling it." I assumed someone made an executive decision about what to throw at us any given day. The imagery I got always seemed to be whatever would hit me hardest right then.

How much did they glean from our assignments and our classroom behavior, and how much were they outright reading our minds? Who knew?

Trix's forehead had furrowed with confusion, and I didn't want to dwell on this subject. Trying to shed light on the school's strangeness was only going to make her more invested, lead her down those dangerous paths. Whatever Elias said, it was a hell of a lot better for me to distract her than to play along with her sleuthing.

"They're nothing all that special, really," I added, and grabbed her hand. "Come here."

I tugged her over to the old carriage house that stood across the lawn from the main college building. Way back in Victorian times, the structure could have held three carriages plus horses in its stalls. These days, from what I'd seen, it wasn't used for much of anything except on rare occasions. Which made it perfect for a brief escape from the school's prying eyes.

Trix followed me with a quizzical expression, but as I kicked the door shut behind us and nudged her up against the wall in the shadow-strewn space inside, a spark lit in her eyes. When I kissed her, she looped her arms around my neck and pulled me closer.

Being this assertive didn't come naturally to me, but she liked it when I took a commanding air—it brought out something more urgent in her too. I liked *that*, even if my own enjoyment of the moment shone only faintly through the numbing layers woven through my body. When I kissed her hard, she kissed me back in kind. When I dipped my hand up under her shirt to cup her breast, she swayed into me with an eager hitch of breath and a fumbling to lift up my own shirt for her access.

She came alive, lit up with desire I could appreciate even if from a sort of distance. I could do that for her. I could bring something good into her existence, focus on someone's happiness other than my own for once in my miserable life.

"I guess this is your way of telling me you're tired of all the lurking and speculating?" she said with a chuckle.

I pressed my mouth to her neck, drinking in her spicy, citrusy scent and the thrum of her pulse. "All work and no play isn't good for anyone," I murmured. "I consider it my duty to help you switch things up. No point in getting bogged down in frustration."

"So you figured you'd offer different sorts of frustration?" Her laugh turned into a gasp when I pinched her nipple.

I slid my other hand down her leg and tucked her thigh against mine. One little heft against the wall and I could have her flush against me, my hardened cock against her sex, just a few layers of fabric between us. "Who says you have to be frustrated?"

"You're getting ambitious today," she teased, but from the way she yanked my mouth back to hers, she didn't mind at all. She traced her fingers over my chest, streaks of muted heat, and I wondered how far we might lose ourselves this time. Distant or not, I wanted it all. I wanted everything. I—

Fuck.

*Was* I thinking about her happiness more than my own? Or was this just a Russian doll of selfishness, the veneer of a larger purpose hiding something so much smaller and pettier. *I* wanted to feel her bucking against me; *I* wanted to know I'd taken her mind away from her quest with these temporary pleasures. What did *she* really want?

I knew the answer to that question without even having to think about it. She wanted to find her brother, to screw over the people who ran this hellish college, and to bring the whole artifice crashing down. She was only letting me divert her because she *was* frustrated and didn't know where to go from here.

Maybe she wouldn't ever get what she wanted, but who the hell was I, really, to decide I knew better?

Or rather, to decide that the approach to the situation that let me feel like I was acting out of generosity while also getting my rocks off however much I could was better than any of the other options I could have taken? Jenson's comments yesterday stung just as much if not more than Elias's did.

If there was any chance at all that she could get free of Roseborne, shouldn't I help her try for that? Instead, I was giving her reasons to stay, painting over the pain with these little interludes so it wouldn't rankle her as much as it should.

The guilt wound up through my chest and made my

lips falter against hers. I eased back from Trix, my heart thumping, my hands still braced against her body.

As her fingers went still against my abdomen, she peered at me with her head cocked. A hint of tension had already come into her stance. She knew how to read that something was wrong even if she couldn't have guessed exactly what.

"Ryo?" she said.

How the hell could I tell her? Every muscle in my body ached to push the doubts aside, lean in, and get right back to the kissing and wherever it would lead. Like a pang of withdrawal that could turn into throbbing agony in no time at all.

And that was exactly why I had to stop.

"We shouldn't be doing this," I said.

She outright stiffened at that, shoving me farther back. My hands fell to my sides.

"And you just decided that all of a sudden?" she said, but there was no humor left in her voice. It'd gone taut with more emotions than I wanted to think about— nothing like the happiness I'd wanted to offer her.

"It's not because of you—it's nothing you did—"

"You aren't seriously giving me the 'It's not you, it's me' speech, are you?"

I didn't know the right thing to tell her. I should have figured this out before—I should have realized I'd been wrong before.

I sucked in a breath and forced myself to look her in the eyes. In those lovely, light green eyes that stared back at me now full of nothing but betrayal. I'd provoked that emotion plenty of times before, but not lately. Never in her. This was going all wrong.

To hell with it. I'd be as honest as I knew how to be.

"It isn't me," I said. "Believe me, I want you, so much. But I'd be the biggest jackass alive if I convinced you to stick around for my benefit when— You've seen what this place is like, Trix. Half of the reason I want you is because you're by far the best thing I've found here. The rest is shit. You don't deserve to be dragged down into that crap."

She crossed her arms over her chest, her gaze still accusing. "I'm here now. And you have no idea what I deserve or don't."

"I think I do. You're not like us. Just the fact that you came here because you wanted to help someone else, already knowing something wasn't quite right, proves it."

"So, what are you saying, exactly?"

I swallowed thickly and motioned toward the building outside. "I've been a distraction. I'd like to be more than that for you. I don't think you're ever going to beat the powers that be or fix everything that's wrong around here, but there's a chance we can at least fix how wrong it is that *you're* here. We can figure out the best way to convince the staff to let you leave—"

"That's what this is about?" She stepped away from me, toward the door. "Even you want to kick me out of here now? If you decided you just weren't that into me, you only had to say so. I didn't ask for the fucking moon."

I blinked at her with the uneasy sense that she was responding to more than my words, to past hurts that I hadn't realized I would scrape up against. "I know. I swear to you, it's not that. I want to see you get out of here so you can have an actual *life*."

"I have a life," she snapped. "It's with Cade. I'm not leaving here without him. So if you actually want to be helpful, you'll tell me how the hell to find him or what happened to him."

My throat constricted. I couldn't tell her, not exactly. And what good would it do if I tried to? He was as trapped here as the rest of us. If she got a hold of even that thread of hope, she'd never leave, no matter how hopeless the situation actually was.

"Trix," I started.

Her expression shuttered. The refusal must have come across in my tone. "If that's the best you've got, I'll take care of it myself. Thanks for nothing."

She stalked out of the carriage house with a slam of the door behind her, leaving me more alone than I'd ever felt in my life.

# CHAPTER SEVENTEEN

*Trix*

When I went up to the dorms after lunch to grab my jacket, Delta was still huddled under the covers like she had been since yesterday morning. I hesitated by my bed, my legs locking.

Everyone kept reminding me that I didn't belong here. I'd intruded on her room and her classes and taken as much help as she'd been willing to offer me… Had some of the consequences I'd faced rubbed off on her? Or was it just a coincidence that in the less than two weeks since I'd arrived, she'd gone from looking a little fragile to languishing in her bed?

Whatever strangeness possessed this school, it had its own balance, and I had to have sent that out of kilter.

I'd been going to wander through the campus woods again and see if I could pick up on anything I'd missed before, but instead, when I reached the main floor, I found myself walking over to the dean's office.

What was the point in pretending this school's set-up was at all normal? The staff knew what they were doing, and they had to realize that by now I'd have figured out something supernatural was going on. Playing along and hoping the pieces would fall into place hadn't worked out so well so far. Maybe it was time to take the bull by the horns.

My hand dropped to my right forearm, tracing the lines of my starburst scar that matched Cade's birthmark to gain a flicker of determination. Then I knocked on the door like I had that first day when I'd only had the barest idea what I was getting into.

Dean Wainhouse opened it a moment later and considered me from his great, gawky height. "We meet again, Miss Corbyn."

I might have smiled at the dry remark if his expression hadn't been so sour otherwise. He definitely didn't look *happy* to see me.

"I have some concerns about the school," I said. "I figured you're the best person to bring them to."

One of his silver eyebrows lifted. "Seeing as you're not officially enrolled at Roseborne, I'm not sure you can expect to have much sway over how we run things here."

Even he wanted to rub in the whole "you don't belong" mantra. The memory of my argument with Ryo yesterday flitted through my head with a clench of my gut. I forced myself to smile anyway. "Well, it does affect the 'official' students too. Do you want to discuss this in the hall or should I come in?"

His lips twitched with the faintest hint of a grimace, but he stepped back to let me in and closed the door behind me. As I walked over to his desk, I scanned the room as quickly but thoroughly as I could, just in case I'd missed something *here* the last time. If anyone had continuous access to that locked basement area, I had to think it'd be the dean.

My gaze settled on an aged wooden box at the corner of his desk. It was so small I hadn't paid much attention to it during my furtive nighttime search—it obviously didn't hold any kind of records. But from the lines and joints that marked its surface, it appeared to be a puzzle box, the kind you could only open with the right combination of movements and pressure points. The kind of place you might hide something small but important if you'd rather not keep it on your person?

Or just a diversion that had nothing to do with the school's main mysteries?

I couldn't get away with poking at it right now. I sank into the chair across from the desk and waited while the dean took his spot on the other side. He didn't bother to sit down. Did he think he was going to intimidate me like that? I leaned back in the chair, shifting to make myself more comfortable.

"One of my roommates is sick," I said. "She's too weak to even get out of bed. She's officially enrolled and all that. I haven't seen any of the staff doing anything to help her."

Wainhouse showed no sign of surprise. "I assure you

that Miss Savas's condition is being monitored, and we'll attend to her as is necessary."

Such warmth and compassion. I eyed him. "I've gotten the impression all of you don't necessarily mind when the students aren't feeling well. I mean, hell, you have a class that's basically for poisoning us and one for shooting arrows at each other. Is this a kind of extended punishment because she didn't perform exactly to a professor's liking?"

"We prefer not to discuss any student's status at the school with their peers for the sake of privacy," the dean said. "If Miss Savas wishes to share her personal situation with you, I'd imagine she's capable of doing that."

"Not if she thinks she'll get in even more trouble." I waved my hand toward the front of the school and the gate beyond it. "She can't even get to classes anymore. Why don't you let her just go home?"

"I'm afraid that's not possible."

I pushed forward in my seat. "Why not? What's the point of this place, anyway? Do you just get off on making people miserable? What have any of them done to deserve this?"

Dean Wainhouse's face stayed impassive. "As I said, we don't discuss students' personal situations. As to the running of the college, that's within our sole discretion. We are quite satisfied with the results so far. Is that all you had to complain about?"

He asked the last question as if I'd been whining like a petulant child instead of raising major concerns about my classmates' well-being. I should have known this wouldn't get me anywhere.

I shoved back the chair and stood up. Anger burned in the back of my throat, but I couldn't see any point in letting that out either. What could I say to him? He didn't care what I thought of him or his school. I couldn't even claim that assholes like him would get what *they* deserved in the end, because I'd seen plenty of assholes get off scot-free.

I didn't manage to keep my mouth completely shut, though. "Everyone has a weak spot."

A glimmer of a smile crossed the dean's lips. "And that applies to you as much as it does anyone. Have a good day, Miss Corbyn."

That was a threat if I'd ever heard one. I walked out fighting a shiver, just as Jenson came sauntering down the hall toward me.

He glanced at me and then the office I'd emerged from, and his mouth tightened at a crooked angle. "Did you figure you'd get anything useful out of him?"

His tone wasn't as mocking as it'd often been before. I hesitated, weighing my response. Something had shifted in the tension between us over the last few days. The last time I'd talked to him, after deciding I wasn't going to take anything he said seriously, he'd responded to my calm retorts with an attitude that had started to feel more playful than accusing.

And then he'd taken off as if I'd slapped him in the face. It'd been pretty weird all around, really, but it suggested there was more going on behind those bright blue eyes than he'd shown earlier.

It was becoming pretty clear there was more going on with *everyone* in this school than I could assume from initial impressions.

"Beggars can't be choosers," I said warily. "Leave no stone unturned. And whatever other clichés apply."

The corners of his eyes crinkled with momentary amusement that I didn't think I was imagining. It disappeared a moment later with a shadow that crossed his face.

"When are you going to learn to let it go?" he said, his voice so gentle that I blinked at him, half expecting to realize I was talking to someone else altogether.

"Let *what* go?" I said. "People are getting hurt. I still don't know what happened to my brother. I know it pisses you off that I'm here, but I can't just walk away from that."

"I— That wasn't—" He made a strangled sound, as if I was somehow being unreasonable. "Just look at how things have gone so far. Think about what they've already put you through. Do you really think it can't get worse?"

"Of course not," I said with rising irritation. "I'm taking that chance. Which is up to me, by the way."

"And I'm *so* sure you're going to save us all. You're never going to find him. He's gone. Why do you think I keep telling you that you should go too?"

"Because you're a jerk who doesn't know how to keep his opinions to himself?" I retorted, taking a step closer to him. "Where's Cade gone? If you know what happened to him, why don't *you* tell me?"

Jenson's expression wavered and then hardened. "I just know he's gone," he said. "Why can't you listen for once?"

"I might when you give me a good reason to." I spun around and stalked toward the front door. I still had another ramble through the woods to make, and at least I had a small hope of getting some kind of useful answer there.

Maybe it was Delta's soft but ragged breaths in the bed next to mine, or maybe it was my frustration that I still felt so far away from Cade after all the time I'd spent here—including another fruitless wander through the woods—but the college's atmosphere was especially eerie that night. In the darkness, a burst of sobs carried through the wall from the room adjacent to ours. The roof creaked. A thump sounded outside, close enough that it might have been just beneath our window. The moaning howl rose up, mournful and ghastly as ever.

I pulled my blanket over my head like Delta had, but the sounds trickled in anyway. Every exhalation turned the air around me uncomfortably humid.

At least an hour must have passed without me getting any closer to sleep when someone in the room let out a choked sound.

At first, peering through the darkness, I couldn't make out which of the beds it'd come from. A breath hissed through gritted teeth, and then Violet sat up, shoving off her covers. She slipped across the room and out the door, favoring her right leg with a more prominent limp than I'd seen before.

Was she getting more messed up too? It'd figure, since other than Ryo, she and Delta were the only students who hadn't outright shunned me. Although I'd gotten the sense she was avoiding me since she'd directed me to the shed the other day. She'd managed to never linger in the same room as me any time I would have had the opportunity to ask questions.

So, I couldn't say it was for entirely selfless reasons that I eased out of bed myself and padded after her.

The hall was empty, but it wasn't as if there was anywhere to go other than into a different bedroom or downstairs. The faint squeak of the bottom step reached my ears, and then a rasp I thought was the bathroom door springing free from its frame. I slunk after her.

Light glowed beneath the bathroom door. I pushed it open tentatively.

Violet's head jerked around. She was standing by the sinks, holding a damp washcloth to the burnt side of her face. When she lowered her hand, ruddy marks had dappled the white fabric. She was bleeding.

"What are you doing here?" she snapped. "I don't need an audience."

She was so obviously in pain that her rebuff didn't sting that deeply. I took a step back, resting my hand on the door. "I just wanted to make sure you're okay. Do you need anything for that?"

"There's nothing you can get that'll help. This is what I have to live with. Why do you care anyway?"

"I don't know. Maybe because I'm trying to be a halfway decent human being."

She glowered at me. "Well, none of the rest of us here are even halfway decent, so you can save the Good Samaritan act for someone else."

All my aggravation with the school and this whole situation boiled over. "Who the hell is such a horrible person they should have to walk around with open wounds on half their body for their whole life? This place is sick, and it's messing with you. You can't just—"

Violet lowered her hand with the cloth to the edge of the sink with a smack that cut me off. "You have no idea what you're talking about. You want to know what I did before I came here? Will that shut you up?"

The vehemence in her voice startled most of the rancor out of me. I still answered truthfully. "I can't promise I'll shut up, but yeah, I'd like to know."

She sighed and turned on the faucet. Cold water streamed over the cloth for several seconds before she turned it off again and returned the cloth to her cheek. She looked at herself in the mirror and then down at the sink.

"They didn't really do this to me," she said in a detached tone. "I did it to myself. My decisions, the people I hurt…"

She was silent for a moment before going on. "There were so many kids at my high school who looked down on me and laughed about my clothes and my hair behind my back, who'd ignore me if I ever tried to talk to them… After a while I got so mad I didn't give a shit about any of them. I looked up on the internet how to make a bomb big enough to take out half the cafeteria, and I put it all together, and I planted it right in the middle of where the worst of them usually sat…"

Her free hand trembled. She gripped the edge of the sink. "Sometimes I still think they deserved that, even if I deserve this too. It didn't work exactly the way I wanted it to. No one died. But a bunch of them were in the hospital for weeks. And I wasn't far enough away. Part of the blast caught me too. I thought it would heal eventually, but no such luck. I'm stuck with it, just like I'm stuck here, because that's who I am."

I stared at her. There'd been plenty of kids who'd hassled me at one school or another, but I couldn't imagine getting to the point where I'd actively have tried to murder them. Even the accident—

I jerked my mind away from that thought. I'd had Cade most of that time. Maybe my mind would have gotten more twisted up if I'd been on my own.

"Is that how it is for everyone?" I ventured. "You all hurt people, or whatever, and that's why you're here? They're punishing you for that?" Delta's story about the girl with the allergy wavered up from my memories. What was Ryo here for? Or Jenson?

Or Cade? My stomach knotted. I knew the most likely answer to that, and I was also the only person who might know he shouldn't really be blamed. It shouldn't have happened at all.

Violet shrugged. "That's one way of looking at it," she said noncommittally.

From the way she and the others always talked about what went on here, I wasn't sure she could give a more definite answer than that.

*What have any of them done to deserve this?* I'd asked Dean Wainhouse this afternoon, and maybe now I had my answer, even if the punishment still seemed to overshadow the crime.

"And you've been stuck here for two years?" I said quietly, remembering what Violet had told me before. Had she been bleeding for her wrongdoings, never allowed to heal, for all that time?

"That's right," she said. "We'll see how much longer I make it."

Those words hung ominously in the silence between us. I wet my lips and couldn't help switching to the other subject that'd been on my mind. "The shed—Cade—was that *his* punishment?"

It couldn't be, could it? If it was, then he'd still be using it. Unless he hadn't "made it" as long as Violet had, whatever that meant.

"Everyone has their own burdens to bear," she said. "He made his decisions."

Her use of the past tense niggled at me. "Is he still *here*, somewhere? You don't have to tell me where, just— If I knew I still had a chance…"

She turned her full gaze on me, the one eye sunken within the mass of scars, the cloud of hair turned even more rumpled by her attempts to sleep, adding an additional wildness to her appearance. "No one has a chance to get out of this. Except maybe you. But I'm starting to think you're too stupid to take it."

The insult didn't bother me as much as it might have from anyone else, in any other context. I wasn't sure she was right about my chances, though. From what she'd just said, I might belong here more than Cade ever had. Yes, I'd come of my own accord, but since then, had the staff realized what crimes *I'd* committed? Would I find myself faced with some everlasting torment once they'd decided on one that was fitting?

Maybe that was the real reason I'd been allowed to stay here in the first place. Roseborne's staff might have uncovered my past right from the start and decided I deserved this as much as anyone else they'd drawn in. For all I knew, they'd spent the last several days observing and considering the best punishment to inflict on me.

The impulse gripped me to tell Violet, to spill the whole damn thing that I'd never admitted a shred of to anyone. Fragments of the memories I'd tried to bury so deep raced through the back of my mind: the shadowy courtyard, the dog's vicious bark, the gasp, the shattering glass.

My hands fisted by my sides, and my stomach balled just as tight. If I opened my mouth, vomit might come out instead. I hadn't really meant to—

But I had. I'd wanted to hurt someone just as badly as Violet had admitted to, and not someone who'd ever hurt me even a little bit.

A wave of dizziness washed over me. I closed my eyes and swallowed down the urge and the memories, and when I opened them again, all that remained was a dull nausea.

"Not stupid," I said, because I felt the need to answer her somehow. "Just stubborn."

She rolled her eyes, but without any real hostility now. "A lot of the time those seem to be the same thing." She shifted the cloth against her face and winced. "If you're done with the interrogation, I'd really rather look after this alone."

"Right. Of course." I didn't have any reason to hang around watching her. Lord only knew how hard it'd been for her to make her own confession to me.

Coming out of the bathroom, I should have turned toward the third-floor stairs, but my feet had ideas of their own. A tug in my chest drew me over to the grand staircase and down, then out under the dark sky with its mix of clouds and stars.

The cold grass nipped at my socked feet. I darted around the building to the shed.

The cot was still there where I'd left it. I sank onto it and pulled the ratty blanket up over me. The hint of Cade's scent tickled into my nose.

When I closed my eyes, I could almost feel his arms around me, like in our secret place in the backyard, like careening on his sled, like the last time he'd really hugged me more than a year ago.

*I'm going to find you,* I promised him silently as my mind drifted toward sleep. *I won't let them make you pay for what I did.*

# CHAPTER EIGHTEEN

*Elias*

I'd thought this moment through with all the consideration I'd given my business plans back in the day, but my pulse still hitched when I spotted Trix walking out of her classroom. I ambled over to join her, aiming to look casual more for the benefit of anyone watching than hers. She hadn't spoken to me since the day she'd confronted me on the lawn, hadn't appeared to pay me any attention at all, so I assumed she'd written me off as a lost cause.

How much could I blame her after the way I'd acted?

"Beatrix," I said, pitching my voice just loud enough to carry over the murmurs in the hall as other students meandered toward their next destinations, but not so loud as to draw excessive attention.

She looked back and stopped when she saw me, her fingers curling around the sleeves of her leather jacket. I couldn't read anything in her expression other than suspicion. I supposed I deserved that too.

"Yes, Elias?" she said as I caught up with her, with a tightness to her tone that suggested she still felt a little awkward calling any supposed teacher by their first name.

My hands were halfway to the lapels of my suit jacket before I caught the nervous impulse to tug it straight, as if it could get much straighter. "I was hoping you'd take a quick walk with me," I said. "We didn't end our last conversation on the best note. I'd like to try to make up for that."

Her skepticism warred with curiosity on her face. I could tell curiosity had won when a gleam came into her light green eyes. "Fine," she said. "Where are we walking?"

I motioned for her to follow me down the stairs. It was as gloomy as ever outside, but I felt less observed out there rather than inside, constricted by the school building's walls.

The damp breeze penetrated my suit in an instant. Trix zipped up her jacket and tucked her hair behind her ears. She was wearing her skirt today, paired with those combat boots in the perfect picture of defiance. When the pleats fluttered in the breeze, I had to make a conscious effort not to admire her leggings-clad thighs.

I drifted on a diagonal course toward the spot where the wall disappeared into the woods. "You wanted me to tell you what I know. I'm afraid there isn't a lot I can say, but I should have been more willing to help before. I'm sorry about that."

She slung her hands in the pockets of her jacket and

looked at me with half a smile. "You admit that you were going out of your way to avoid me, then? What was that all about? I wouldn't have badgered you at all if you'd just treated me like all the other students."

As I probably should have realized. But it was better that I'd fucked up, because my fuck-up and her calling me on it had forced me to see that steering clear of her wasn't the right approach after all. Not for the man I wanted to be now.

"It's complicated," I said. "Can we leave it at that?"

"No, I don't think so. What's so complicated? You hardly even know me."

"Well, I..." I groped for a suitable answer. "You remind me of someone else. Someone with whom I regret my past interactions. If I'm being honest, I was worried I'd end up falling into the same pattern."

"So, you blamed me for your past mistakes. Very nice." She narrowed her eyes at me. "What kind of 'pattern' are we—"

The breeze shifted with a sudden gust, and she had to swipe at her skirt to stop it from flipping upward. I jerked my gaze from there to her face, but the look of consternation she'd made was so familiar it sent a twinge through my chest too.

She glanced back at me a second too soon and must have caught some of that emotion in my expression. I yanked my attention away, to the trees ahead of us, but I couldn't contain a hard swallow that might have been audible.

Trix tsked under her breath. "Have you been

fraternizing with the students more than you're supposed to?"

Yes and no. "I'm not really— It's not the same," I said. "I ended up here the same way as pretty much everyone else."

"Then why do they have you teaching a class?"

"Because…" Answering that question was even harder.

But Trix must have seen and heard enough by now to fill in the blanks, especially with my hesitation. Her eyes widened with understanding. "Is that your punishment? Teaching a bizarro math class? I'd give you my sympathies, but from what I've seen, it could be a lot worse."

"It is," I found I was able to say, perhaps more momentously than I'd have preferred to if I'd known the words would actually come out. When I made myself turn to Trix again, she was studying me with that gaze that saw so much more than I should have wanted it to.

"That's not all they're doing to you," she filled in.

I didn't answer, which was probably answer enough. She sucked her lower lip under her teeth to worry at it, and my eyes were automatically drawn to the movement. She caught that slip too.

"I remind you of a girl you liked," she said, stopping and peering up at me. "Enough that it scared you. Am I less scary now that you've seen I'm not her? Is that why we're having this talk?"

I hesitated. "You remind me of her because of the ways you're the same. And what scares me is thinking that you could meet the same fate she did. I'm still scared of that. If I can stop it from happening, I'll do whatever I can."

"This is about seeing me as some pathetic thing in need of saving, then."

A laugh sputtered out of me. "No. Not at all. Pathetic is the last word I'd use to describe you."

She considered me a moment longer. Then she stepped closer, setting her hand on my arm. Letting her fingers trail over the smooth fabric of the suit's sleeve. Watching my reaction with absolute intentness. The pressure of her touch only seeped faintly through my clothes, but that contact combined with her closeness was enough to spark a tingling that shot straight to my groin.

"Trix," I said, my voice abruptly hoarse.

She couldn't know what she was doing to me, but she must have been able to observe enough. She cocked her head, mischief and bemusement dancing together in her eyes. "So that's what it takes for you to say my name properly. You need to stop getting crushes on your students, Elias. Even if you're only sort of a teacher, it doesn't really seem appropriate."

"I'm not acting on it," I pointed out. We wouldn't get into how much I might want to, or how much I had or hadn't in the past.

"Would you if I wanted you to?"

Her tone was sly, but her body tensed, just slightly, at the same time, as if she wasn't sure she wanted to hear my answer, whatever it might be. A different sort of twinge ran through me, tenderness rather than lust. I couldn't forget that under the defiant front, she had plenty of her own vulnerabilities.

I set my hand over hers where it was still resting on my

arm and eased it away from me, but kept a gentle hold on it. "If circumstances were different," I said. "But they're not. You shouldn't be here at all, Trix. Your life is waiting for you out there." I nodded toward the other side of the wall.

Her jaw clenched in an instant. "My God. Is that the only thing anyone can think of to say to me? 'You don't belong here.' 'Just leave already.' 'Do it for your own good.' How selfish do you all think I am?"

Not hardly selfish enough. "That's not what I'm saying. You told me before that I couldn't do anything for you because I wasn't trying to, and that was true. I'm trying now. I can do *this*. The worst thing you could do is chain yourself to Roseborne if you have the option of getting out."

"Because no one else can ever leave and there's no hope for any of you and blah blah blah." She backed up, pulling her hand from mine. "I've heard the whole spiel. I'm starting to think it's part of the game here. Are the staff pulling your strings, making you all parrot this shit to stir up doubts in my head? It's not working."

I shook my head. "This is just me. If you're hearing it from other people, will you consider that it might be because we all know what we're talking about?"

"Right." She let out a rough chuckle. "What did you do that was so horrible, exactly, Elias? Somehow I don't think you were setting off any bombs or pummeling people in the street."

She wanted to know, did she? Why the hell shouldn't I

tell her? Soon enough it wouldn't matter, one way or another.

"You want to know what I was like before I came here?" I said, because I could answer that question if not the one she'd actually asked.

"Yeah. Convince me of how irredeemable you are." She folded her arms over her chest.

I stared right back at her, not letting my gaze waver. "I was an unrepentant prick. I thought I was better than everyone around me, that I was going to do better things, and that because of that, I was justified in stepping on anyone who was even partly in my way to boost myself up. I tossed aside people who'd been real friends to me. I fucked people over when it came to school and jobs they needed and a hell of a lot more. Collateral damage. And if that doesn't sound bad enough, the last time I shoved someone aside, they died because of it. And for a hell of a long time I managed to convince myself it was their own fault for being a victim."

Trix hadn't looked away, but she winced toward the end of my tirade. "What did you think you were going to do that was so great while you were screwing up everyone else's lives?" she asked.

I shrugged. "I had plenty of business plans. Launch a start-up, change the world. I was on my way. But it wasn't worth shit in the end, because here I am."

I could have pointed the finger at my grandfather and blamed a hell of a lot of it on him, but how would that help Trix—or me? The anger was there, the prickling sense of betrayal toward the man who'd raised me in his image, but ultimately the decisions I'd made had been mine. The fact that I could own that now might be the only reason I was still anywhere at all.

"You had a lot bigger plans than I did." Trix tugged at her hair again, her gaze sliding away from me. I had the sudden impression that I was losing her, as much as I'd had her attention at all. That any second she might walk away assuming everything I'd said to try to help her was bullshit.

"It doesn't matter," I said. "Whatever plans you had, they're still yours. You can't— The longer you stay here— Come with me."

I swung around with a beckoning gesture, half afraid she wouldn't follow. But she did, keeping a small but careful distance, the rest of the way across the lawn to the wall with its covering of dark leaves and thorns. I let my hand hover by the rose blooming there, its petals still fully vibrant and unblemished.

"Lean in," I said. "Look at it, smell it, absorb everything you can about it. And tell me who it makes you think of."

She gave me an odd look as I stepped back to give her room, but she did as I'd suggested. Resting her fingers lightly on the outer petals, she lowered her head to the flower. As she breathed in deeply, she closed her eyes. Then she opened them again, studying its structure. With another deep inhalation, her brow knit.

"I—I don't know *why*—Jenson Wynter just popped into my head."

"Let's try another." I motioned her farther along the

wall, all the way to the next rose. This one was starting to fade and crinkle along the edges of its petals. Trix leaned in again. This time she lingered over the blossom for a little longer.

"I don't know his name," she said quietly when she straightened up. "But there's this guy who was sitting in front of me in Tolerance class…"

I nodded. She stared at the rose a moment longer and then started forward. "Okay, let's see the next one."

We passed into the shadows of the forest. Roses still bloomed along the wall there at random intervals where enough hazy sunlight reached them through both the clouds and the trees. The fresh blossom she encountered next made her mention a girl in her composition class.

She slowed as we came up on the fourth in this experiment, the one I'd been leading her to all along. The petals had wilted in on themselves, the whole flower drooping under the weight of its decline. A brown brittleness was seeping through it. It looked as though one sharp gust of wind might be enough to scatter those petals completely.

Trix balked for a second before she forced herself to approach it. Her shoulders stayed rigid as she brought her nose to the blossom. They stiffened even more a few moments later as the impression must have filtered through her senses. She drew back with an expression so haunted I had the impulse to take this all back somehow, as if I could.

"That's Delta," she murmured. "She's— The rose— Is it hurting her, or just reflecting, or—" She glanced at me.

"You can't tell me, can you? If *you* even know. You just figured out whatever this is by stumbling on it like you're showing me now."

I spread my hands in a vaguely helpless gesture.

She released a huff of breath and looked around. "Do I have one, then? Where's that?"

"I don't know," I said, which answered both questions at once.

Her gaze returned to me. "But you're worried it'll happen. What will that mean for me?"

"I don't know," I had to admit again. Other than I'd watched over a dozen of those roses shrivel up in the time since I'd recognized that they were more than roses, and I'd yet to see any re-bloom.

"This is ridiculous. They're *roses*. It shouldn't— Fuck." She raked a hand back through her hair. "What the hell am I supposed to do with this?"

It would have felt too cruel to repeat the same refrain. "That's up to you," I said instead.

From her choked guffaw, that answer hadn't done much of anything to reassure her. All I could do was hope she understood why this mattered so much—why she should get the hell out of here before her life was tied to a single fragile flower blooming on the wall that shut in all the rest of us.

# CHAPTER NINETEEN

*Trix*

Early morning light looked even more anemic when delivered through the layer of gray cloud that I was starting to realize always hung over the college, except maybe at night. The feeble glow turned the rose I was examining faded in turn, even though the texture of the petals showed no sign of withering yet.

It'd taken me most of yesterday to wrap my head around what Elias had shown me. After dinner, I'd come out on my own and walked the wall in both directions until I came to stretches where there appeared to be no more roses ahead at all. The campus spread out for so many acres I was leery of trying to follow the full circuit. Even after I turned around, the uneasy sense lingered that I could wander for hours and never emerge on the other side of the woods.

Every rose I stopped and inspected held a faint echo of

a presence. I doubted I'd have even noticed if Elias hadn't made a point of telling me to watch for it. With a casual glance and sniff, the impression would have darted by without clicking in my mind.

But because I was looking for it, I knew when I'd found Ryo's rose, deeply red and just starting to crinkle along the edges of the petals. An image flitted through my head of green-streaked hair and dark brown eyes, the relaxed tones of his voice, the warm smell of him like sunbaked sand. In combination with the way he'd pushed me away the day before, the sensations had brought an uncomfortable lump into my throat.

I'd found Elias's rose too, off past the carriage house and the rusting posts of the badminton court. His had sent a prickle of uneasiness through me for a different reason: the petals were curling with age, splotched with brown here and there. Nowhere near as sickly as Delta's blossom, but clearly heading in that direction.

What would happen to him when it withered more? How long did the students here get before they met the fate he'd said he was trying to save me from? Violet had said she'd been here more than two years, and her rose had looked nearly as healthy as Jenson's, just a tiny bit dimpled with age.

I hadn't come across a rose that felt like *me*. But late in the evening, following the wall along the edge of the campus woods, I'd reached a fresh bloom with a brownish vein seeping through one outer petal that sent Cade's presence singing through me. That was the one I'd come back to this morning.

The discolored vein seemed ominous, but nothing else about the rose appeared to be deteriorating. What exactly that meant, I wasn't sure. Would the rose linger on if he wasn't on campus anymore?

At the very least, I thought I could assume he was alive and reasonably well. As well as anyone could be staying at Roseborne College.

I'd thought seeing the flower a second time in a different light might shake some new revelations loose, but it gave off only the same gauzy impressions as before. I didn't dare touch the petals in case I damaged them somehow and that hurt Cade. With the limited supplies I had here, I couldn't think of any strategy that would definitely make any of them healthier. If I experimented, there was a whole lot more at stake than when I'd tended to the Monroes' garden.

How were the students and the roses bound together? Was it a one-way relationship, what happened to the flower affecting the person or vice versa, or did the energy flow both ways?

Studying the bloom in front of me, a whisper of Cade's voice trickled up not from the rose but from my memories. *We didn't need silly things like flowers to know how much we matter to each other, right, Baby Bea? We're better than that.*

And then that day when I'd gone out back to find half the roses on the bush I'd been so carefully encouraging back into health chopped off. Cade bundling them in a cone of paper at the kitchen counter. *I figured you wouldn't mind. They last so much longer fresh. Gotta treat this girl right.*

He'd given me a wink and a peck to my cheek when I hadn't protested. *You're the best, Trix.* And off he'd gone to his car to pick her up for their six-month anniversary date.

I closed my eyes against the uncomfortable prickling that came with the memories. I'd been so desperately, ragingly hurt and yet equally torn up because I didn't have any good reason to be, and—

I'd have given anything to be back in that moment, any moment, before this place had sucked him in. I wouldn't take what I'd had for granted this time.

There were no time machines here, though. I lingered by the rose for several minutes longer, with less hope as each second slipped by, and then trekked back to the school building in time for breakfast.

Delta had made it down this time, although she sat at her table with shoulders hunched and only picked at her food. Her face looked outright haggard. She'd seemed to have friends or at least people happy to shoot the breeze with her before, but the seats on either side of and across from her stayed empty, as if whatever she had might be catching. When I moved toward her, she glared at me, so I let her be.

If she was well enough to come downstairs, maybe she was on her way to recovery. She'd made it very clear earlier that she didn't want me hovering over her.

No classes ran on the weekends, thank God, but we still had our cleaning duties. I found myself in the main foyer vacuuming the rug with a machine I suspected was twice as old as I was while two of the other girls polished every inch of the suits of armor at the base of the staircase, even removing the massive shields to work those over on both sides. Another rubbed lemony-smelling wood polish into the banisters and the wall paneling.

Every sweep across the room took me into view of the staff hallway and the door at its end. In my mind's eye, I crept down the stairs on the other side to the padlocked basement entrance.

What were my chances of breaking through there if I couldn't get my hands on the key? The clasp and the lock had been too thick for me to hope that any of the tools I'd seen in the shed would cut through the metal. There was always the trick of tackling the hinge side rather than the lock itself, but when I thought back to my explorations, the hinges hadn't been visible. The door must open inward. I had no access from this side.

There had been a small ax in the shed, dappled with rust so probably not that sharp anymore. I could always chop my way right through the door… as if I was likely to get all the way through before the professors caught on. The racket that would make, they wouldn't need any special senses to realize something was wrong.

The problem gnawed at me. For all I knew, Cade was locked away down there, just one simple door standing between me and him.

When I'd put the vacuum away, I came back to find one of the other girls struggling to mount the shield back on the suit of armor she'd polished. I leapt to take some of the weight while she maneuvered it into the right position.

I'd seen her in class before but hadn't caught her name. Which one of the roses I'd checked yesterday evening had she been tied to? I couldn't remember.

"Hey," I said casually, hoping my help would have bought me some good will. "Have you ever seen any signs that there are students living at the school who sleep somewhere other than the dorms?"

She looked me in the eye for the first time then, swiping a stray lock of hair back from her eyes. "You've really got to give it up already."

Her tone set off a spark of irritation in my chest. "I don't really think that's up to you. Why should you care anyway? It was just a simple question."

"I care because I'm sick of your stupid face," the girl shot back. She grabbed her polishing rag and stalked off before I could come up with a remotely appropriate response.

All right then. Someone had a stick or three up her ass.

The girl who'd been cleaning the other suit of armor had taken off too. The one with the wood polish appeared to be just finishing up at the top of the bannister. I stepped back from the armor to take in the space and make sure we hadn't missed anything—I'd prefer to skip any future migraines unless they were for a good cause, thanks—and a familiar voice reached my ears from down the hall past the cafeteria.

"Give me a break, man."

That sounded like Ryo. Frowning, I eased over to the stairs and peeked over the now-lemon-scented banister.

It *was* my formerly friendly punk dude—and the jerk

he'd defended me from before. Ryo and Jenson were standing just past the arched entryway beyond the row of portraits, Ryo's shoulders tensed and Jenson with his arms crossed over his narrow chest.

"Is it a difficult question?" the taller guy said in the companionable tone I'd heard him turn on for plenty of people other than me. "Or are you not so gung-ho about the whole 'working together for the greater good' thing after all?"

"I'm doing my part," Ryo said. "Even though it feels like shit. How much have you changed *your* tune?"

"All it took for me was a little tweaking. No big deal. Forgive me for asking." Jenson held up his hands with a slanted smile and sauntered away.

Ryo ducked his head and muttered what sounded like a curse. My hand tightened on the banister as I watched, debating whether to approach him. A trickle of shamed heat washed over my skin when I remembered the last time we'd spoken. Him telling me how he liked me so much that he *had* to kick me to the curb and encourage me to get the hell out of here, to give up on the whole reason I'd come here at all.

Another voice traveled like a ghost from the more distant past, somehow managing to sound sweet and mocking at the same time. *Things were never meant to keep going like this, Baby Bea. I thought you knew that. You're my* sister. *You really want me to forget that, throw away everything else we've got together?*

*No*, I'd said, every time, again and again. *Of course not.* Because what else could I say? I *should* have known.

Sometimes people needed you in certain ways, and sometimes they didn't, but that had nothing to do with the love and loyalty that was always there.

That back and forth wasn't anything like this situation with Ryo anyway. There'd been no love or loyalty between us in the first place, just two people indulging in a little mutual chemistry. Or what I'd thought was mutual, anyway.

He exhaled slowly and turned to head toward me, and that made up my mind. I slipped down the stairs to meet him by the portraits.

He stopped in his tracks, his eyes brightening and his jaw clenching at the same time. "Trix."

"Hey." My tongue momentarily tangled. I didn't need to get flustered over this guy. There was a perfectly quick and simple way to see if I should bother talking to him at all. "Have you gotten over your heroic impulses? I think we left a little business unfinished in the carriage house."

A flicker of what looked like hunger passed through his expression. For a second, I thought he'd give me his easy smile and motion for me to follow him outside. Then his stance went as rigid as it'd been when he was talking to Jenson.

"It wasn't just an impulse," he said. "And I was telling the truth. The most important thing to me is seeing you out of here safe. I was an idiot before."

A little of my earlier annoyance flared inside me. "An idiot for wanting to make out with me?"

"No. Well, maybe. For putting that first. Trix…"

I groped for something else to say that might knock

him out of this ridiculous mood he'd gotten stuck in. "I found out about the roses. I've seen Cade's—and yours, and, well, everyone's. It's so crazy. Just having someone to talk to who isn't going to laugh in my face or turn their back on me would be nice."

Ryo's mouth tightened. He glanced away, his eyebrow ring glinting in the chandelier's light. Apparently he couldn't offer even that much. Well, I guessed that was all I needed to know.

"You have to see," he started, and I was already shaking my head.

"I do, and I wish I didn't. So glad I could help you get your rocks off while you were up for that."

I turned my back on him before he could do the same to me again with another half-assed excuse. That was the way you had to handle things if you didn't want to get stomped all over. Nothing had really changed. My whole life, I'd been able to count the number of people I could count on with one finger.

But what if that person hadn't been right to count on me?

# CHAPTER TWENTY

*Jenson*

Somehow or other, the burned Violet had gotten her hands on what looked like a genuine joint. She had the balls to smoke it within view of the school's front doors, leaning back against the brick wall as if she hadn't a care in the world. As if the wounded side of her face and the back of her hand didn't glower nearly as starkly as the red end of the rolled paper between her fingers. It was a bit of an odd sight.

I'd never been one to let an opportunity pass me by, though, and Violet hadn't been that tough a nut to crack. Even if "nut" was a pretty accurate word to describe her. I'd figured out pretty quickly that her sense of humor had a dark streak that ran as deep as the Mariana Trench, and she got a lot more offended by people pussyfooting around her obvious scars than showing they weren't fazed by the things.

I meandered over with a grin already in place. "Playing with fire, huh? Haven't you had enough of living dangerously? Or are you waiting to see if you can get both sides to match?"

Violet let out a bark of a laugh and switched the joint to her other hand. "Of all the things that scare me these days, I think you can safely assume flames aren't one of them."

I propped myself against the wall a couple of feet away from her, giving her the personal space I figured she needed. "Where'd you score that anyway?"

"A new kid turned up this morning," she said. "I managed to bum it off him. I think he took pity on my horrible torment. These do come in handy every now and then." She gestured to the scarred side of her face and blew a stream of smoke into the dimming late-afternoon light.

"Never get between a girl and her spliff," I said glibly, but my stomach had sunk. Every time a fresh face turned up at the college, it felt as if one of the thorns on that damned rosebush had jabbed into my gut.

We all deserved to be here, no doubt about that, but the newbies didn't know that yet. They had no idea what they were in for.

Violet tapped off a bit of ash and looked sideways at me. "I'm surprised you haven't already noticed the kid, convinced him you're his new best friend, and conned him into handing over the rest of his stash. Been a little distracted lately?"

Her dry tone told me she already knew the answer to that question. She didn't talk a whole lot, but that just meant she heard and saw plenty while everyone else was caught up in their own dramas.

I waved her question away. "I've been focused on self-improvement. Eyes on your own page and all that. So, is it any good?"

She made a face at the joint. "As far as I can tell, Roseborne has already leached all the fun stuff out of it. I'm literally blowing smoke. But it's kind of nice just going through the motions after all this time. Like I'm living a normal life for a moment. Almost." She let out a rough chuckle. "You want a drag?"

"After that stunning recommendation? Ah, why not?"

I held out my hand, and she passed the joint to me. I'd never been much of a smoker of any sort—when you relied on a quick tongue and quicker thinking to keep you ahead, addling your brains with illicit substances wasn't exactly smart—but every now and then I'd indulged as a way of blending in or ingratiating myself. People liked watching other people give in to the same vices they had.

Thank you, Mother Dearest, for that lesson.

I sucked in a cautious wisp of smoke and determined that Violet's assessment had been right. I didn't even catch the burnt prickling down my throat that a cigarette would have offered, let alone the hint of a buzz to come. But the heat of the rolled paper in my hand and the thin smoke congealing in my mouth came with a weird sort of enjoyment.

Violet had earned the thing fair and square. I took another brief drag and handed it back to her. I'd heard enough of her story in our classes to know that back when we'd been in the real world, she'd have hated the hell out of who I'd been then, if she'd known me. No point in stirring up old resentments by acting entitled.

"Doesn't seem like she's going anywhere," Violet remarked.

I didn't need to ask who she was talking about. "What makes you say that?"

"Oh, I don't know, the fact that she's still here? She gets top marks in stubbornness, anyway. In it to the end, even if it kills her."

She couldn't make that last sentence sound anything but dire. We both knew it wasn't an "if" but a certainty.

With a shake of her head, Violet pushed off the wall. "I'm starting to see why you like her, though," she said, and ambled off without giving me a chance to confirm or deny, apparently having reached her socializing limit for the day.

I stayed where I was for a moment, soaking in what little sun penetrated the clouds and wrestling with the annoyance and guilt her words had provoked. Just as I turned to go back inside, Trix herself came striding out.

Her gaze slid over me, and her mouth set in a firm line. She marched onward with a resolute air as if she'd decided I wasn't worth her attention, but halfway past me she appeared to reconsider. She swung around and planted her feet in the grass with her hands on her hips.

"What were you bugging Ryo about this morning?"

I blinked at her. Of all the things I might have imagined she'd ask me, that wasn't one of them. "Pardon?"

She rolled her eyes. "In the hall by the cafeteria. You

were hassling him about something to do with 'working together' and 'doing his part.'"

Ah. For once my particular affliction worked in my favor. "School project," I said with utter confidence. "He didn't seem to be pulling his weight, and I didn't want to see how the profs would react if we don't deliver. How's that your business anyway?"

"I don't know." She eyed me. "It's funny how suddenly you're working on a 'project' together right when he's also decided to start telling me to take off like you've been saying all along. Do you have something on him—did you put him up to that somehow?"

What kind of an asshole did she take me for? Okay, I wouldn't deny that I *could* be an asshole and had been plenty of times in the past, but I wasn't a blackmailer, for fuck's sake.

"Sure," I said. "Because the guy couldn't possibly have a mind of his own. Did you ever consider maybe he just wised up and realized I had the right idea all along?"

"Don't pretend you haven't had it in for me since the moment I set foot on campus," Trix retorted. "You knew he was hanging out with me. I wouldn't listen to you, so why not turn whoever you could against me to add to the pressure?"

The playful spirit that had started to emerge when we'd dueled the last couple times had disappeared under what was by all appearances genuine anger… and hurt? Because Ryo had mattered that much to her? Or because she hadn't thought *I* would stoop that low?

My heart squeezed despite myself. This caustic back

and forth wasn't getting us anywhere. I'd already decided to trash that tactic. So why the hell did I keep finding myself falling back into the same dynamic? I was the master of adapting to the situation. Trix shouldn't be any different.

But she was, and I had one major limitation I'd never had to work around outside these walls.

The frustration of it constricted my throat. I dragged in a breath. "Do you really think I'm just out to hurt you?"

My voice came out strained despite my best attempt at keeping my cool. Trix's expression didn't exactly soften, but confusion took the edge off her hostility. "If you're not, you're making a pretty good show of it anyway," she said.

That was fair. And it might be the whole problem. Why would she believe the other guys when they told her it was best for her to leave when she'd already heard me spouting the same thing like a jackass? She didn't associate that suggestion with concern—she thought of it as an attack. Because of me.

How the fuck did I fix that?

An idea wriggled into my brain—something I'd discovered by accident in my first month on campus and never experimented with further because of the consequences. Because I hadn't cared enough about anything to endure those consequences. But I owed Trix. If there was a chance it'd show her that I wasn't just some prick, that underneath the jabs I'd always wanted what was best for her too even if I'd screwed that up...

Yeah, that was worth whatever hell rained down on me after.

Resolve tensed my posture. I tipped my head toward the college building. "Will you come with me? Let me show you something? Trust me just a little, please."

Uncertainty showed all through her stance, but the "please" seemed to loosen it. She moved stiffly, but she did move. "I don't trust you. But if you've got something you think I need to see, fine."

She was prepared for the worst, clearly. Not a great starting point, but one I'd set myself up for, so I could hardly complain.

I headed back into the school and aimed for the music room at a casual pace. If any of the professors happened to be around and glanced over, I didn't want them suspecting my intent before I'd gotten my chance. The light thump of Trix's combat boots told me she was right behind me.

No one was in the music room, naturally, because no one was ever in here except to conduct the weekly cleanings. Trix's brow knit as she looked around the room. I turned the lock on the knob, not expecting it to keep the professors out but hoping it'd buy me at least a moment extra when even a matter of seconds could be critical. Then I went over to the wall where the guitars were hung.

"Are you going to serenade me?" Trix said with blatant skepticism. "I thought playing the instruments was off-limits."

"Who says I can't break a rule here and there?" My gaze settled on the acoustic with the rosewood sides and spruce top, like the one I'd set my sights on years ago beyond these walls. Maybe the exact sound quality didn't matter all that much right now, but who knew when I'd play again? I might as well make the most of the experience for both of us.

As soon as I started working the guitar over, my time would be running out. I hefted it and swung it under my right arm, already plucking the strings to check the tuning.

"Have you ever heard that music speaks from the soul?" I said as I gave one knob and then another a quick twist. "A wise man once told me it's the highest truth there is."

"Jenson," Trix said, looking at me as if I'd broken out in purple polka dots, but I couldn't afford to wait and discuss this any further.

I might be rusty from more than a year without practice, but I'd played enough before for the chords of the song I'd chosen to spill from my fingers into the strings with only the slightest fumbling. It felt so *good* to hear the music pouring out, and so awful at the same time to know that in essence this was me saying good-bye to the girl in front of me.

An ache spread behind my ribs. I looked into Trix's face, wanting to memorize it in case this worked, hoping she could read in mine how much I meant this even if they were someone else's words. My mouth opened to launch straight into the chorus, because that might be all I had time for.

The song vibrated up my throat.

"And all I can see

Is that you're out of reach
Meant to go where I can't follow
So all I can do
Is wish the best to you
And do my best to hide my sorrow
Find your dream out there without me
I'll give it all up to see you go free."

Trix stared back at me, frozen in place. She still looked confused, but a hint of a flush had come into her cheeks too.

She was listening—that was all that really mattered. She was giving me this chance despite all the good will I'd already thrown away.

For a second, I thought I might get to dive into one of the verses after all or repeat the chorus for emphasis. Exhilaration tickled up inside me with the strummed melody. I inhaled deeply—

—and pain sliced me open from sternum to gut like a knife wrenched through a fish's belly.

I sputtered and flinched so hard the guitar slipped from my grasp to bang on the floor. The agony radiated through the rest of me so sharply and swiftly that I didn't even have the capacity to regret the damage I might have done to that fine instrument.

My knees wobbled, and my arms snapped tight around my belly. I wasn't actually bleeding, but I felt as if all my innards were about to splatter across the floor.

I'd made my choice, and here was the retribution, swift as always.

# CHAPTER TWENTY-ONE

*Trix*

Jenson doubled over so abruptly that the smack of the guitar against the floor hit me like a slap to the face. The groan that carried from his lips was the total opposite to the passionately melodic voice he'd poured into his song just moments before. I hadn't known what to make of his performance —had been standing, still absorbing it and trying to understand how the guy who'd shown so much rancor toward me could be making this apparent statement of devotion. His collapse didn't answer any of my questions, but it did propel me into action.

"Jenson!" I dashed over to him and knelt down where he'd fallen to his knees, clutching his belly. My hand moved toward his shoulder instinctively and then clenched. Would he even want to be touched in his current state?

He coughed and shuddered at the same time. All the color had leached from his already pale face. I opened my mouth and closed it again against all the questions I wanted to ask that seemed so pointless. He obviously wasn't okay. I wasn't sure he could manage to speak to tell me what he needed, if there even was anything I could do that would help.

"Do you want to lie down?" I settled on. "I can get—" I cast around for anything that could serve to make the floor more comfortable, but the music room didn't offer much along those lines.

Then it didn't matter anyway, because the door whipped open, and Professor Marsden swept into the room.

The sight of the Tolerance professor, petite and ringlet-haired but with eyes hard as flint as she took us in, brought back an echo of both my queasiness in her class and the headache that had struck me when I'd fled it. I shifted to shield Jenson instinctively, as if she might have come to pour some potion down his throat and mess him up even more.

Marsden didn't even let on that she'd noticed my maneuvering. She glided around me as if I barely mattered at all and reached for Jenson's arm.

"You don't look so well, Mr. Wynter," she said in that sharply bright voice. "Let's get you to the infirmary for treatment, shall we?"

Jenson stumbled as she propelled him to his feet. The woman must have been stronger than she looked, because even though he had nearly a foot in height on her, she managed to hold him up through his swaying and walk him to the door.

I stalked after them, not planning on letting Jenson out of my sight until I was sure she wasn't going to do even more damage to him. But when I stepped into the hall, Dean Wainhouse, Professor Hubert, and Professor Roth were waiting. They stepped neatly between me and Marsden to block my way.

"Let me go with him," I said, my fingers curling into my palms. "I need to make sure he's okay."

A cluster of students drifted toward us. It was just about dinnertime—they must have been heading to the cafeteria when they'd noticed the confrontation. I spotted Elias amid the others, watching with a frown, before I jerked my gaze back to the professors.

"Mr. Wynter will be properly looked after," Dean Wainhouse said in his gravelly voice. "I believe we have other, more serious matters to discuss."

More serious than a guy collapsing in a sudden fit? I tried to step between the two professors, but they closed ranks even more tightly. Professor Marsden had already hauled Jenson out of view. I thought I heard a choked breath from the direction they'd gone. Chances were their "looking after" wouldn't really help him.

"Can we discuss them tomorrow?" I said, craning my neck.

"I'm afraid not." The dean exchanged a look with Hubert and Roth. Rather than beckoning me over to his office, he launched into his piece right there with the audience we'd already gained.

"The consensus among the staff is that you're not fitting in well here at Roseborne, Miss Corbyn. Our college does not appear suited for your disposition, nor do you appear to be achieving any goals you had in coming here. We can have someone escort you off campus and arrange suitable transportation to get you home in the morning."

I stared at him as the words sunk in. I'd thought that if I decided I wanted to leave that it'd be a battle even though I wasn't their usual sort of student. It'd never occurred to me that they might drop the offer in my lap.

"About time," someone muttered in the growing crowd of onlookers. I sought out Elias again, but his expression showed nothing but relief. So fucking glad I might be leaving.

My body had already balked. No way, no how. The professors knew I was a threat, that I might uncover more than I had already—

Or was that really it? Jenson's pained groan resonated through my memory. Delta wasn't in the crowd—she'd probably retreated back to her bed to lie there as the sickness crept through her. How many other people might my actions have hurt without my even knowing about it?

It wasn't as if I hadn't proven I could do a hell of a lot of harm without meaning to before. Had I made anything better for *anyone* by challenging the status quo here, or only screwed up the situation more?

"Well?" Professor Hubert said imperiously, and I realized they were waiting for an answer. Our audience was too.

"Just go already," someone else said with a huff. No one said a word to suggest they'd want me to stay. How could I kid myself that I was doing anything for them when all they wanted was to see the back of me?

How could I be sure I was helping Cade rather than increasing his suffering?

My gaze darted back to the hall that led to the infirmary. Jenson had been telling me to go too, but he'd been trying to get across more than that right now. I didn't understand why he'd felt he needed to express it with a song or what he'd felt was so urgent that it was worth the punishment he must have known he'd face, but it had mattered to him that he make his point. In that brief moment while he'd been singing, he'd looked at me like I was the only person left in the whole world.

"I have to think about it," I said, shifting my weight to one side to divert the professors' attention. "I need to talk to Jenson."

I darted the other way, managing to scoot past them before they recovered from my feint. It was only a short dash down the hall to the infirmary room where I'd been "looked after" following my own painful spell in Archery. But my boots thudded against the floor almost as loud as my heart was pounding in my ears, and they must have alerted Professor Marsden.

She appeared in the doorway, jerking the door shut behind her. "The patient needs his rest."

Right, I was so sure they were only concerned about Jenson's well-being, when they were the ones who'd struck him down with whatever dark powers they possessed.

The dean and the other professors were hustling over. My legs locked where I stood. "I'm not making any decisions until I can talk to Jenson. Now or later, if he's too sick right now. It's up to you."

And it was, more than they were likely to admit out loud. If they could turn on the agony in a matter of seconds, presumably they could turn it off too.

Dean Wainhouse folded his arms over his chest with a stern look he aimed down his hooked nose, but then he jerked his head toward the door. "See if he wants to speak to you, then."

I stepped toward the door. Professor Marsden grimaced, but she eased out of my way. I opened it a crack to peer inside. "Jenson?"

He was lying on his side on the narrow cot, facing away from me, toward the wall. At the sound of my voice, his shoulders stiffened. He didn't turn around. Uneasiness congealed in my stomach.

"What do you want, Trix?" he asked in a weary voice.

"I— Are you all right? If there's something more you wanted to say to me—"

"What more could I say at this point? Why are you talking to me when they've just given you your way out?"

He must have heard the conversation from the hallway while the infirmary door was open. My hand tightened around the doorknob. "There's got to be more to it than that. You wouldn't have—"

"Don't worry about that," he snapped, cutting me off. "Just go, Trix. That's all I've been telling you. I don't want you around. Even your brother doesn't want you around.

Do you really think if he cared half as much about you as you do about him that he wouldn't have found some way to see you? *No one* wants you around. So just get the hell out."

I winced, my hand dropping. The door clicked shut. I looked at it in a daze for a long moment, the queasy churning inside me taking on a sharper edge that pinched my gut.

Did Jenson actually know that Cade was capable of seeing me, talking to me, if he decided to? That he was purposefully avoiding me? Was *that* what everyone here had been waiting for me to find out—that the guy I'd come to save was too done with me to want my help?

It couldn't— Cade had always said—

Unless he'd figured out that it was my fault he was here at all. That everything was my fault. I should have been happy for him—I should have wanted him to be happy—and instead I...

I closed my eyes against the swell of horror.

It might not be true. Jenson had been a jerk more often than not. But that didn't mean he was lying now. And even if Cade didn't hate me, what had I really done for him or anyone here? There was so much I still couldn't grasp hold of, and every time I thought I was close to answers, the situation flipped on its head all over again.

Maybe I'd been stupid to think I could tackle this whole problem on my own. If I left, now that I had a better idea what I was facing, I could regroup—call on the police like I'd meant to before, round up whatever other assistance I could get. It wouldn't be giving up. It'd just be taking a realistic approach.

The thought still made my stomach lurch. I had to grit my teeth for a second before I turned to the dean. The words snagged in my throat before I could force them out.

"All right. I'll go tomorrow morning."

Several little whoops went up from our audience of students. I held back another wince. They were outright cheering to hear I was going. That was all I really needed to know, wasn't it?

"You've made the best choice for all involved," Dean Wainhouse said with a shallow nod, just to rub it in. "We'll see that you're on your way in good time."

He and the professors pulled back. The other students were already wandering away into the cafeteria. I stayed where I was, every part of me so clenched up I might as well have been locked in place.

The thought of trying to choke down one more awful dinner while everyone around me celebrated my impending departure made me even more nauseated. When I finally pushed myself into motion, I passed the cafeteria and headed straight up the stairs to the dorms.

I hadn't brought much here with me, but I guessed I might as well make sure I had it all packed up. Maybe think about whether there was anything I could grab to take with me to use as proof when I went to the police or whoever. Of course, what could I get away with taking that the professors wouldn't notice before they saw me off?

What would even convince a bunch of cops that the

staff here were torturing their students? Was my word going to be enough?

As I trudged up the stairs, I could already see in the back of my mind how they'd look me over and laugh and tell me to stop wasting their time. When had anyone who'd been supposed to look out for people like us, the discards and the rejects, ever actually come through? Even when I'd been a kid, no teacher or counselor had seen the signs and intervened. They hadn't *wanted* to believe anything was wrong, to bring that trouble into their lives.

I'd just—I'd figure it out. I would. Even if I had no idea how. It had to be easier once I'd gotten away from this place and the horrors that pressed in from every side, right?

Delta was curled up under the covers on her bed, as I'd expected. The slow rhythm of her ragged breaths suggested she'd at least managed to fall asleep despite whatever discomfort she was in.

I took one of the changes of clothes out of the chest under my bed and stuffed it back in my knapsack. The other outfit I'd wear tomorrow. I plugged in my phone so I'd have a full charge once I finally had service again.

As I glanced around for other odds and ends, my gaze caught on a small object nestled in the middle of my pillow. I sat down on the bed and picked the thing up with careful fingers.

It was a flower, but not a real one. A makeshift blossom formed out of scraps of metal and wire twisted together into something shockingly delicate. The whole thing could fit in the hollow of my palm.

While people downstairs had been cheering, while Jenson had all but spat in my face, someone had been leaving me a gift.

My fingers closed around it. The edges of the petals dug into my skin, but the pain sharpened my thoughts. Even as a lump filled my throat, a trickle of resolve rose up through the hopelessness that had overwhelmed me.

I'd been looking at this all wrong.

A sudden urgency propelled me to my feet and out the door.

# CHAPTER TWENTY-TWO

*Ryo*

There was a moment some evenings, right as the sun was just finishing setting, when the clouds started to part before the last sheen of daylight had quite left the sky. Just a glimmer, rosy or gold, but seeing it shored up what strength I had inside me.

Tonight it was just a flicker of lilac-purple before the sky dulled with the falling dusk. I tucked it away in my memory as I sat on the edge of the abandoned pool, leaning back on my hands. The rough, cracked concrete bit into my fingers. I punctuated the moment with occasional kicks of my heels against the pool wall, as if those hollow thumps would prove something about my deserving to be here.

I didn't want to think about anything beyond this moment. Especially not tomorrow morning and what I would lose, or the fact that I was a selfish jerk for hating that I was going to lose it. Whatever gods there were knew plenty of people existed beyond these walls who deserved *her* and could appreciate her more than I did.

We'd done it. I'd never thought I'd end up allying myself with Elias or Jenson, let alone both of them, but maybe I should have reached out to them sooner. I just hadn't really wanted to give up this one thing. It'd been easier to believe the situation was hopeless.

At least I'd done the right thing this once before I'd dragged yet another person I cared about down with me.

Footsteps rustled through the grass. Figuring it was a random classmate wandering by, I didn't bother to look around until they'd almost reached me. At the sight of Trix approaching, my heart skipped a beat.

She hunkered down next to me, letting her legs dangle into the empty pool like mine were. "I checked too many places before it occurred to me to look out here. I should have thought of it sooner."

"I'll admit I'm fairly predictable," I said, mostly to say something other than all the questions and pleas I really ought to shove down inside.

She rested her hand in her lap, palm-up, holding the little flower I'd fashioned from bits I'd found in the carriage house. "Thank you. Was this supposed to be a good-bye gift?"

I swallowed hard. "No. I mean, you can see it as one, but I left it before I knew. I… I didn't enjoy how our last conversations went, even if I needed to say the things I did. Making that was an admittedly somewhat pathetic attempt at showing I said them because you matter to me, not because you don't."

"I don't think it's pathetic." Her fingers closed around the metal flower. She tucked it into her pocket and looked at me. "I'm not used to people trying to help me. I *do* have plenty of experience with assholes jerking me around, sometimes while pretending it's really for my own good. So, strangely enough, I tend to assume the latter is happening rather than the former."

"I don't think *that's* strange." I let myself meet her eyes. "I'm glad you're getting out of here, but I'm also not. More the first part, though. It'll be fun imagining the havoc you're going to wreak out there in the real world."

She hummed to herself, the slightest smile curving the corners of her mouth. "Not to disappoint you or anything, but I've actually had some second thoughts about that."

My pulse outright lurched. "Trix, you *have* to take this chance—"

She held up her hand to stop me. "I know why you're saying that. And maybe I still will. But the decision isn't just about me—what I want, or what's 'best' for me, or any of that. You tried to help me, and I think Elias and Jenson did too, and you risked a lot doing that. Maybe more than I even understand. I don't care what you did that brought you here or what the professors think they're punishing you for. None of what they're doing here is right."

I wasn't sure I agreed with that, but whether I did or not was beside the point. "The difference is, we're stuck. You can't do anything to change that."

"You can't know that for sure. You didn't think even I could get out to begin with, did you?" She turned to face the western sky, tucking back a strand of hair that the cool breeze had snatched. "There's at least one more thing I haven't tried yet. I've got until tomorrow morning at the very least. We'll see where that gets me. If I find any reason to hope that I can push farther than I have already, I'm telling the dean I've changed my mind."

There was no real competition between the sensations dueling in my chest. The potent pang of horror that she might give up her freedom in part for me easily overwhelmed the muffled joy of knowing that *I* mattered to *her* that much, despite everything. But I clung to the joy anyway, because the tone of her voice allowed for no argument.

"I'd never ask you to do that," I started anyway.

"Of course not. That's why I'm not asking your permission."

"You know, if you do leave, you could still do something for me. I don't know if they're freaked out or glad to be rid of me, but my parents must have wondered why I've gone completely off the radar for so long." For all I knew they'd even come looking for me like Trix had for Cade, but hadn't managed to get past the school's protections, as must have been the case for just about everyone. "If you could look them up and just let them know that I'm okay—enough—and I hope they can move on from—" I halted at the haunted look that had come over Trix's face. "What?"

"I assumed you knew. I guess there's no way you

could." She swiped her hand across her mouth. "I have no idea how they manage it, but the way the school seems to shield itself—everyone forgets. That they ever knew you, that you even existed. My own foster parents who had me and Cade for five years thought I was pulling their leg when I tried to talk to them about him. His friends completely blanked. That was *why* I came out this way—it was so obvious something really weird was going on."

*Everyone forgets.* I had a sudden vision of my parents and little brother sitting around the kitchen table back home, eating a peaceful dinner with soft smiles and playful laughter, like those hazy memories from back in my childhood before I'd turned everything sour. The thought twisted my gut, but not in an entirely unpleasant way. Erasing me might be the best thing that could have happened to them—to everyone who'd known me.

"But you remembered Cade," I said.

"Yeah. I've got no idea why their voodoo didn't work on me."

My throat closed up for a second, which was ridiculous, because he was her *brother*, foster or not. But still. "You must have had something really special. You were so close to each other they couldn't touch that bond."

Her head bowed. The dim light of dusk turned her hair the deeper orange of autumn leaves. "I know I probably seem a little crazy, going through all this to find him, but he's *always* been there for me, right from the start. He stood up for me and listened to me and made me feel like I mattered to someone when I didn't have anyone else. Even if there were times— Hell, I only had a home to leave because he figured out some illegal stuff our foster parents were into and used that as leverage so they didn't kick us out as soon as we each turned eighteen."

"I'm sure you were there for him just as much, if current events are anything to go by."

"I tried. With him being older and better at dealing with people most of the time than I am, I couldn't really pay him back quite as much. But I did my best." That hint of a smile came back. "There was one time—when he was sixteen and first found the evidence of the crap our foster parents were into, our foster dad flipped his shit and came at him like he was going to bash him to pieces. I didn't even think; I just jumped in between them. Those first swings he was already making messed my head up so bad I ended up in the hospital for a couple of days. But it stopped him wailing on Cade."

My hands balled at the thought of anyone hurting Trix like that. "And you wanted to keep living with those assholes after that?"

She shrugged. "Better the devil you know? They were my fourth family. Others were worse. And once we had that dirt on them, they had to be more careful. Cade had it all set up. Even after he left to come here, even after they forgot he'd existed, it was enough to protect me. He was going through God knows what here and still looking after me at the same time. And that whole time—"

She cut herself off again, her back tensing. Things she wasn't ready to talk about, at least with me. But watching her, hearing the devotion and regret in her voice, a sort of determination welled up inside me.

She'd come all this way. She was going to be making a decision that might decide the course of her entire life tomorrow. She deserved to know exactly what she'd be leaving behind or staying for.

I got to my feet. "I think there's something you should see before you do anything else."

Trix looked up at me, puzzled and then with a glimmer of hope in her eyes. More than I wanted her to have. But I couldn't tell her what to be prepared for. I wasn't even totally sure I'd find what I was looking for.

She followed me across the lawn to the edge of the woods. When I moved to step between the trees, she hesitated.

"It's all right," I said. "I wouldn't be suggesting this if I thought there was anything in here that could really hurt you."

"Okay." She dragged in a breath. "It's silly. I just— When I went into the forest at night before, it felt like someone was messing with my head."

Messing with it pretty badly if it was enough for this girl to balk. I held out my hand to her, which seemed like a poor offering at best, but she took it and twined her fingers tightly with mine.

In the daytime, we wouldn't have had much of a chance. Either he slept or simply had enough awareness to steer clear of anyone who came wandering. Once it got dark, it was a different story. I'd heard stories from the newer students who'd dare each other to come out and face "the beast." I'd ventured out myself once just for the sake of seeing. The encounters always seemed to happen around the same spot.

I headed right toward the thickest section at the center of the woods. As the dusk dwindled beneath the canopy of leaves, Trix took out her phone for extra light. She glanced at me curiously now and then, but didn't push for answers. I guessed she'd learned that lesson about how things worked at Roseborne awfully fast.

An owl swooped by us with a flutter of its feathers and then hooted from a distance. A rotten branch let out a low creaking as it swayed in the breeze. We passed a tall, mossy boulder that served as a landmark; I swerved a little to the right to adjust our course. Then, from up ahead but not that far, a ragged howl split the air.

Trix's fingers tightened around mine. I tugged her along gently until we reached a patch between the trees that was a little more open, if hardly large enough to call it anything like a clearing. There, I grabbed a fallen branch from the ground. I rapped it against a nearby tree trunk, paused, and banged at the tree again. Drawing attention.

"Ryo," Trix said, hugging herself. "Are you sure—"

Pebbles rattled nearby with a huff of breath that was mostly snarl. A dark form emerged from the shadows several feet from where we stood.

I couldn't have said what kind of animal it was meant to be most like, if the powers that be had given it all that much thought. Its body was as large as a bear's, with fur as coarse and shaggy and shoulders as broad, but its head sported conical ears and an extended snout that were much more wolf-like. Like no animal I'd ever seen, uneven fangs jutted from its jaws to crisscross against its muzzle. Its gangly limbs looked overly jointed, as if they could bend in ways no living being should be able to. Short but jagged claws glinted on its paws in the light from Trix's phone.

She sucked in a breath, a tremor running through her. The creature swung its monstrous head toward her.

"Easy there," I said in my steadiest voice. "Let's just—"

Before I had time to register what was happening, the thing's muscles bunched. It launched itself straight at Trix.

# CHAPTER TWENTY-THREE

*Trix*

The monster in the woods hurled itself at me so suddenly I barely managed to move. My feet stumbled backward, the phone slipped from my fingers, and then its massive paws were smacking into my chest, knocking me to the ground.

"Trix!" Ryo shouted, barely audible through the panicked rush of my pulse past my ears. "Hey, stop it! Get off her!"

The creature loomed over me as it pinned me in place, its mouth opening with a knife-like snicking of its interlocking teeth. Hot breath laced with a rancid scent flooded my face. My spine ached where my back had hit the forest floor. Terror held me momentarily frozen, afraid that if I tried to fight I'd only provoke the thing more.

It peered down at me, the light from my fallen phone shining off the pale eyes embedded in its mass of thick black fur. Pale *gray* eyes, just a shade shy of silver and weirdly human-looking. Weirdly… familiar.

My breath caught in my throat. Ryo shoved the monster, and it snapped at him with a clack of its teeth, but it bounded off me. As I scrambled into a sitting position, braced to flee, it hunched into a crouch a few feet away. My gaze skipped down over its body to its left front leg. To the streaks of white fur that cut through the darkness like a starburst.

My stomach flipped over. I moved to get to my feet, and the creature whirled. It charged off into the night as swiftly as it'd leapt at us. I stared after it, a shiver rippling through me from head to toe. The chill it brought sank deep into my chest.

"It had— That was—" I couldn't quite force the words out. My voice shook.

Ryo touched my arm tentatively, his expression fraught, looking as if he expected me to scream at him for bringing me here. "I'm so sorry. I didn't think it—he— I thought you'd be fine because of who you are. It's never hurt anyone *that* badly, but if I'd realized there was any chance—"

He'd stumbled, started to call the thing *he*. The pieces clicked together even more solidly in my head.

"That was Cade," I said, barely managing more than a whisper. "That's what the school did to him. It turned him into that… that monster."

Those had been my brother's eyes staring at me from the creature's face. That had been his birthmark, the one

I'd carved into my own skin, marking its foreleg. My hand rose to brush over the scarred spot on my arm.

"I wanted to show you," Ryo said, equally quiet. "I figured you should know. I just didn't— Come on, we should head back toward the school. He never comes that close to the buildings, but as long as we're in his territory, I'm not sure he won't come at you—or me—again."

He bent to pick up my phone and then took my arm again. His fingers curled around my elbow. I balked for a second, gazing off in the direction the beast—my brother—had gone. But the guy beside me could clearly tell me more about what had happened than I'd get from the thing that had just attacked me. My back still throbbed from the fall.

I turned and walked with Ryo back the way we'd come. My thoughts kept spinning in my head. Not all of the pieces totally fit. What about the painting in the hall? What about the cot in the shed?

"He wasn't always like that," I said into the hush of the forest after a long silence. "He couldn't have been. He used to be at the school like the rest of you."

"I'm not sure of the details," Ryo said. "And there's only so much I can say anyway. But—from what I understand, it developed gradually. He'd change and change back, and over time it lasted longer."

So Cade hadn't just transformed into that thing once and been done with it? He'd had to shift back and forth, over and over… Somehow I didn't think the college had let that be an easy process. It was meant as a punishment. God.

I could picture it with the shreds of his history here I did have. He'd been able to attend classes at first, to sleep in the dorms too, presumably. And then as he'd been trapped in that horrible form for more and more time, he'd retreated to the forest. He must have kept his humanity during the night for the longest—he'd started sleeping in the shed rather than interrupt his roommates' sleep by coming and going from the dorm at odd hours…

"Does he change back at all now?" I asked as the thought struck me. "Or is he just always… like that?"

Ryo grimaced. "I don't know. I haven't seen him looking like *him* in a few months now." He glanced over at me. "I wish I could have told you something to prepare you better—I can't imagine how you feel."

I put my hand over his where he was still holding my arm. "It's okay. I'm just glad someone finally let me know, one way or another."

What did it mean for Cade that he'd been warped into that *thing*? Was there any way to turn him back into his old self, no matter what I did? I'd thought if I could fight back, take on the college and what it stood for, maybe I could break the control the staff wielded over this place, but the monster they'd turned him into was a hell of a lot more extreme than refusing to let some burns heal or forcing Elias to teach a frustrating class.

Whatever power this place had, it was even more potent than I'd suspected.

I couldn't talk to Cade about it, even in a one-sided conversation. I wasn't sure he'd recognized me at all. If they'd given him monstrous impulses to go with that form, then who knew how deeply the man he'd been was locked away underneath?

Maybe it wasn't so surprising that everyone had avoided trying to answer my questions about him. They couldn't have told me directly, and they might have thought it'd be worse if I knew than if I simply thought he'd disappeared.

If I went to the professors and told them what had really happened, why he'd acted the way he had—that I'd been responsible for the whole thing, really—was there any chance they'd reverse his fate? Let him go free? I'd be trading places with him, but by all rights, it should have been me here in the first place. The methods they used for bringing in new "students" were obviously flawed.

I didn't trust any of the staff to have an honest conversation with me, though. They were just as likely to suck me into their psycho system without changing a thing about Cade's situation as they were to show any kind of compassion. I didn't have the leverage to make deals with people who could transform a human man into a monstrous beast.

"Lots of deep thoughts?" Ryo said lightly as we stepped from the forest onto the lawn. "Not that I blame you. But if you want to talk anything through—I'll do my best."

He'd been waiting patiently in silence for most of that walk. I swallowed hard, looking at the school building ahead of us, every bone in my body resisting the idea of setting foot inside those walls where the staff ruled so completely.

"Is there somewhere we can talk that's even a little private?" I asked.

One side of his mouth quirked up, even though he still looked mostly sad. "We can always make use of the carriage house. I didn't get to show you much of it last time."

We gave the school a wide berth, slipping through the faint glow that spilled from the lit bedroom windows. The door to the carriage house opened easily. The smells of aged wood and leather washed over me, more comforting than I'd expected.

Ryo led me over to the hall that ran along the length of the building. One side held doors to the stalls that I guessed must have housed cars rather than carriages in more recent years… however recently Roseborne had admitted long-term visitors in cars onto campus. Old tack—harnesses and bridles, some of it looking on the verge of disintegrating—hung between the doors. A line of benches stood along the opposite wall, mostly wood but with the seats covered by a thin layer of cracked leather.

I sank into one of those, Ryo beside me. He dropped my arm and then didn't seem to know what to do with his hands. His awkwardness and the concern shining from his golden eyes brought a pang of affection into my chest.

He was trying so hard to do right by me, for no reason other than he wanted to, even though he'd just met me. Like Cade had all those years ago, except even Cade had the motivation of knowing he'd be stuck with me for at least as long as our foster parents held on to both of us.

Ryo could have easily shunned me like the rest of the students had.

Maybe he would still shun me if he knew the whole story. If he knew I'd been as much responsible for turning my brother into that monster as the school was. If he ever found out…

I didn't want to think about that. As selfish as it might be, I let myself lean toward him, tipping my head against his shoulder. Just like that, his stance relaxed. He eased his arm around my back and rested his chin against my hair.

"I'm glad I know," I said, "but I have no idea what to do about it. Every time I find out something new about this place, it just gets worse, and bigger, and crazier…"

"I've been here for years, and I haven't seen any way out," Ryo said. "You shouldn't expect yourself to manage it. I don't know how this all started or where the professors got their power, but they have a hell of a lot of it. That's why I think you should go while you can. What good does it do staying here if all that accomplishes in the end is ruining your life too?"

"I can't just walk away now that I know. Even if I leave, I'll still be thinking about what's happening here. I'll still be trying to figure out a way to break you all out of this."

"Or maybe you'll forget like everyone else, finally," Ryo said softly. "And get the peace you deserve."

My stomach twisted. "What if I don't deserve it?"

He eased back far enough to look me in the eyes. "Whatever you've done in your life, whatever mistakes you've made, there's no way they're that much worse than what the rest of us here have done. And you seem to think *we* deserve better. Why the hell wouldn't you?"

Because they'd paid for it plenty and I hadn't? Because I already knew the college had claimed at least one person unfairly? But the man in front of me was gazing at me with so much faith that I could let those protests slide, just for the moment.

There hadn't been many people in my life who'd ever believed in me. Looking back at him, all I could feel was how much I needed that right now, here on the precipice of taking what would probably be the biggest risk of my life. How much I wanted to show him what it meant to me.

There was one simple way to do that, one that I'd enjoy just as much as he would. I raised my hand to his cheek and drew him in for a kiss.

He kissed me back in that eagerly tender way of his. I let my fingers trail up into his hair, tangling in the smooth strands. Ryo kissed me harder, his tongue teasing across the seam of my lips until they parted. It delved into my mouth, twining around my own tongue. A wave of giddy anticipation rolled through me.

Ryo tugged me closer to him, and I took the encouragement as an excuse to swivel around completely, straddling his lap. Our mouths only slipped apart for a second before we were kissing again with even more passion.

My hands roamed up under his shirt, and he took the cue to make his own explorations. The skillful fingers that had crafted the little metal flower stroked over my bra and urged my nipples to peaks as quivers of pleasure raced through my chest.

It wasn't making love, but it was making me feel incredibly damn good, and that was the most I'd ever been able to ask for. Ryo had told me before that he didn't expect any kind of commitment from me. It might be the last bit of pleasure I got to take in my life, so I'd better make the most of it.

I shifted on his lap, grinding against the bulge that had hardened behind the fly of his jeans. Ryo's breath hitched. As I traced the firm muscles of his chest, he unhooked my bra with a flick of his fingers and dipped his hands beneath it. With just a few caresses, he brought a gasp to my lips. Then he tugged my shirt up and tore his mouth from mine to bring it to the peak of my breast.

I gripped his head as the heat of his mouth flooded me with bliss. He sucked my nipple hard and worked it over with his tongue and the tips of his teeth until I was moaning and squirming against him. Then he performed the same magic on the other side. I swayed against him, my fingertips skimming over his scalp, my sex aching where it brushed against his erection.

As he encouraged another jolt of pleasure from my breast, I eased my hand down between us to stroke his cock directly. In a matter of seconds, I'd unzipped him to remove the most obvious obstacle. His erection sprang free with a couple more tugs. I smiled through a sigh as I gripped the silkily stiff flesh.

Freeing myself took a little more effort. When Ryo raised

his head to pepper kisses across my collarbone, I yanked at the zipper of my own pants and wriggled out of them as quickly as I could without pulling too far away from him. Claiming his mouth again, I rubbed against him through my panties, squeezing the base of his cock until a groan escaped him.

Ryo drew back and looked up at me, his eyes gone heavy-lidded and even darker than before. "Are you sure?" he murmured.

"I've got an implant," I said. "And I'm clean. As long as you are too…" I assumed condoms weren't easy to come by around here, but then, maybe it was ridiculous to even be thinking about STDs in a bizarre world where the weather never changed and everyone's life was bound to a freaking rose.

"I'm good," he said. "But that's not what I meant. You've been through a lot, just in the last few hours—"

I lowered my head so my forehead brushed his. "That's why I need this. I want you. I want to remember how alive I am." A sudden doubt unfurled in my chest. "Unless *you* don't—"

"No." He cupped my cheek. "I want you too. I'll always want you."

"And you have me." I kissed him and yanked my panties to the side. I was so wet already that I slid down onto him with only the faintest burn that turned almost instantly into a sear of pleasure.

"Trix," Ryo mumbled against my lips, and let out another groan as I rose and sank over him. His hips bucked up to meet my rhythm. As we rocked together in deeper and deeper pulses, he clutched my thigh, connecting our bodies that much more determinedly.

The bliss built so fast through my core that it was almost bittersweet, but I couldn't bring myself to slow down. We crashed into each other over and over, the pleasure taking me higher, our breaths ragged between chaotic kisses. I soared farther with each thrust inside me. Then ecstasy burst like fireworks behind my eyes, ringing through me and flooding out every other emotion.

Ryo gripped me tighter as I clenched around him. A tremor raced through his body as he reached his own release. He pulled me to him, our bodies hot and damp with sweat in the cool air, and pressed a kiss to my cheek.

And in that moment I couldn't help thinking it was a shame that "always" might not be more than another day.

# CHAPTER TWENTY-FOUR

*Trix*

Ryo and I parted ways on the second floor between the two sets of stairs. He brushed a kiss to my lips with no sign of the awkwardness that sometimes followed an intense hookup like we'd just shared.

"You do what you have to do," he said. "Just remember that you don't owe me anything."

"Hey." I poked him in the chest. "Same goes for you."

He grinned at me in a way I was starting to find way more adorable than was probably wise and headed up to his dorm. I turned in the opposite direction.

I wasn't planning on actually sleeping yet, but if I was going to pull off what I'd planned to attempt tonight, I should probably make a show of going to bed. The thought of making this last-ditch effort made me so restless it was probably better I lay down and at least pretended to rest while giving my nerves a chance to settle. If it was a little early to turn in, I didn't think any of my roommates would care that much.

I reached the top of the stairs to the girls' dorms and hesitated there. A few of the students were clustered around the door to my bedroom, leaning past the doorframe and then murmuring to each other. A thread of uneasiness pierced through my chest.

"What's going on?" I asked, walking over.

The girls didn't answer, just eased back to let me through. I stepped inside, my heart already sinking, to find Violet and a couple of my other roommates standing around Delta's bed. The covers were drawn back from Delta's face, her red hair stark against the white pillow beneath it, but I couldn't see much else between the observers.

"She's gone," Violet said, and glanced up. Her mouth tightened when she saw me.

One of the other girls who I thought might be younger than me wrung her hands. "What do we do? I didn't think she'd really— She'd only been sick for a few days—"

The girl between her and Violet shook her head. "It'd been creeping up on her for a while. The staff probably already know, but if it makes you feel better, you can go look for the dean or one of the professors. They'll take her out when they're ready." Her tone suggested she didn't expect them to be ready with any urgency.

I hugged myself as I approached the bed. Delta's cheeks had caved in on themselves, almost as dark as the rings that surrounded her eyes. Those eyes stared blankly straight ahead, already starting to glaze. Her lips, pale and cracked, hung slightly open, as if she'd been dragging in one last breath when her body had failed her.

No. I wasn't sure how much I'd even *liked* Delta, but I'd never have wished this on her. Just this morning, she'd made it to breakfast. She'd seemed like she might be getting better, not worse. How could—

I spun around before I'd even known I was going to move. If I could just—if there was some way—

The fractured thoughts chased me down the stairs and all the way out onto the darkened lawn. Just enough moonlight seeped between the strewn clouds overhead that I didn't need my phone to guide me. I hurried along the wall and into the sparser stretch of forest there, my chest getting tighter by the second around my racing heart.

I recognized the spot from the jagged stump where a tree had toppled sometime in recent months. Just past that, at about my shoulder height on the wall, I should find Delta's rose…

It wasn't there. Leaning close, I made out a couple of narrow, pointed leaves, yellowed and shriveled, where the blossom had been. Shit. I dropped to my knees, fumbling across the uneven ground below in the dark.

My fingers brushed something dry and delicate that gave a soft rasp as it shifted. I froze and peered closer.

A small heap of brown petals lay at the base of the rosebush, a few of them still clinging tenuously together.

Their edges had cracked, one already crumbled into smaller fragments.

My stomach lurched. I braced my hands against the earth, willing down the urge to vomit.

No one could fix that flower, no matter how green a thumb they had. There was no restoring that bloom to life. If I was being honest with myself, I doubted I could have rejuvenated it even if I'd started trying when I'd first seen it. And that was assuming it was growing in a natural way and not as much dictated by the whims of the staff as everything else here appeared to be.

I stood up on shaky legs. The image of Delta's wasted face remained in the back of my mind. When I closed my eyes, it only loomed more vividly.

She couldn't have been that much older than me— none of the students looked like they were older than their mid-twenties, and most of them younger than that. Was that how it went for everyone? They were trapped here for however long the college decided their punishment should last and cut down completely after just a few years?

How much longer did Cade have? Ryo? Any of them?

How short would the rest of *my* life be if I stayed?

Twigs crackled underfoot. I looked up to see Elias making his way over, his expression solemn, looking weirdly formal in one of those suits he always wore.

He stopped beside me and took in the bush and then the petals on the ground. "I heard about Delta. I thought you might be out here."

His rose had been starting to crinkle up. Had he already prepared himself to go the same way she had?

"It's awful," I said. "Like the life was just drained out of her. I wish there was something I could have done…" I turned back to the rosebush. "I'm good with plants out there in the regular world, you know. That's what I want to do when I've saved up enough: start some kind of business setting up people's gardens for them and looking after them."

"These aren't your standard roses," Elias said. "Sun and fertilizer aren't going to stop them from dying. And you shouldn't be worrying about this anyway. You're leaving tomorrow, like you're supposed to. It's okay, Trix. No one here expected you to save us."

Delta definitely hadn't. I remembered her annoyance at my shows of concern. But Elias's words twisted me up inside with a different memory: seeing the relief on his face when I'd accepted the dean's offer. He hadn't spoken a word to me.

I gave him a defiant look. "I think I might have changed my mind about leaving."

His lips jerked into a frown. "Over this? You couldn't have done anything to stop it, I promise you. You have to think—"

I held up my hand to stop him and then rested it carefully on his chest over the lapel of his suit jacket. Over the spot where his heart would be thumping. Maybe it was selfish, but I wanted to see the flicker of heat that would light in his eyes like it had when I'd stepped close to him before. To remind myself that *some* part of him liked having me here.

"I don't *have* to do anything for anyone," I said. "I got

overwhelmed in the moment and thought I'd screwed everything up, but I'm not ready to totally give up. Thank you for trying to protect me, though, even if I didn't always like how you were going about it."

"That really is all I've been trying to do. Protect you." His voice came out low and a little rough, and a tingle shot over my skin, as if I hadn't just taken my fill of another guy less than two hours ago. It was hard not to wonder just how much passion might lurk behind that starched exterior.

I tipped my head toward the deeper forest. "I know about Cade now too. Ryo showed me. I don't know if I can leave without at least trying to talk to him, even if he can't understand with… what they've done to him."

Elias considered me for a long moment, his jaw working. Then he said, "Half past midnight."

"What?"

"Half past midnight," he repeated, tilting his head in the same direction I had. His mouth set as if he regretted the words, but understanding struck me. I might be able to talk to Cade properly if I found him then.

I checked my phone. It was barely ten. Way too much time to kill. But then, I needed to wait until pretty late before I attempted my next gambit anyway.

"Thank you," I said, wondering how he knew. I had seen him coming back to the dorms awfully late that one night. What brought him wandering around campus into the early hours of the morning?

From what I knew of this place, it couldn't be anything good.

An impulse gripped me that I didn't give myself a chance to deny. I shifted forward and wrapped my arms around Elias's solid frame, hugging him with my head against his shoulder. He inhaled with a start and then hugged me back, one hand stroking over my hair. For all the rigid strength coiled through his body, I caught a tremor of something more vulnerable underneath. A warm scent drifted up from his body, like dark coffee laced with a hint of sugar, exactly the way I liked it.

My thoughts tripped back to the third guy I'd had a close encounter with this evening, the one who'd literally put himself through agony to say his piece. The memory of the last words Jenson had spoken to me made my body tense up, but the business between us didn't feel finished.

I had time. I should see what he'd say when half the school's staff wasn't hovering over us.

I drew back from Elias, and he stepped back farther, as if he didn't trust himself if he stayed in arm's reach. "I guess tomorrow morning we'll see where I'm at," I said with a faint smile.

He nodded. "Be careful."

As if I could be, really.

When I reached the school, the whole place was dark, even the third floor windows. Had the staff collected Delta's body? One of our roommates had seemed to think they wouldn't be in any hurry. Maybe they liked leaving that glimpse into the students' future on display to remind them of the fate they'd all face. I shivered as I stepped into the foyer.

There was no sign of any of the staff moving around

on the ground floor. It occurred to me on my way down the hall to the infirmary that Jenson might have been moved back to his dorm bedroom if he'd recovered enough. How would I reach him if he was up there? I didn't even know which bedroom he'd be in, not to mention the various other students to contend with who might object to me being on the guys' side.

But when I nudged open the infirmary door, Jenson's form was immediately visible in the dim light that crept through the room's tiny window, lying on his side on the cot like he had been when I'd looked in on him before.

The door clicked into place behind me, and he stirred, rolling onto his back. At the sight of me, he sat right up— and didn't manage to hide a wince. He obviously wasn't completely recovered yet.

"What are you doing here, Trix?" he whispered. It was hard to tell whether his tone sounded more worried or annoyed.

"I needed to see you," I said. "Even if *you* don't want to say anything else to me, there are some things I need to say to you."

Tucking in his legs under the blanket, he eyed me warily as I crossed the small room. I hesitated and perched on the edge of the cot by his feet. My fingers curled around the metal frame.

I dragged in a breath. "You've been a jerk to me most of the time since I got here. But after what happened this afternoon, I can't believe it's because you hate me. I think maybe you've been trying to protect me in your own stupid way like Ryo and Elias were. And that—that matters a lot to me, even if I wish you hadn't been such an ass about it. I'm going to stay at least a little longer and do what I can to protect you all too, and no jabs you take at me are going to change that. So, can you just be honest with me for a minute or two? What's really going on, Jenson?"

A ragged chuckle fell from his lips. He tipped back his head to gaze up at the ceiling as if searching for answers there. When he looked at me again, his mouth was twisted halfway between a smile and a grimace. "Are you ever going to give up?"

"Not because of anything *you* say," I said.

"Trix, if I could, I—" He shut his mouth and exhaled in a rush. Then he met my eyes, more serious and intent than I'd ever seen him before. "Your shirt is white."

I glanced down at my very dark navy top. "What?"

He went on, each sentence coming a little faster than the last. "It's the middle of the day. We're in the library. I have three arms. Two plus two is five. I could walk out the front gate right now if I wanted to."

Where the hell was he going with all this? "Jenson," I started, bewildered, and he leaned forward to hold my gaze even more urgently.

"I can tell the truth," he said, each word like a punch.

I stared at him for several seconds as my mind whirled —and gradually connected the dots. Everything he'd said in that random string of sentences was a lie. Including that last statement?

A chill pooled in my gut. "That's your punishment?" I said quietly. "You can't say anything true? But—"

Surely I'd have noticed if *everything* he'd ever said in my presence was a lie? I searched back through my memories, trying to pinpoint a moment that would make *this* a lie, and the certainty only settled deeper and heavier in my belly.

"You're always saying things like questions," I said, studying his expression. "Questions can't be true or false. Or you'd tell me to do something. That's an order, not a fact. But you did sometimes just state things…"

Things like that Cade didn't want me around. That *Jenson* didn't want me around. Which had been lies too. Convenient lies when he'd wanted to push me to accept the dean's offer.

"And the song?" I went on. "You can be honest if you're technically just performing?"

He shrugged, which might have been as close to a direct answer as he could give me. Then he said, even softer than before, "Don't think I ever *wanted* to hurt you, Trix."

A lump rose in my throat. I scooted closer to him along the edge of the cot, not knowing what to say. He raised his hand to rest his fingers against the side of my face, a strange mix of trepidation and affection coloring his expression, as if he still wasn't sure whether to welcome me or shove me away.

So much emotion had reverberated from his voice when he'd sung that song to me. A song about his sorrow at seeing me go, about being willing to give up everything for me. I couldn't assume that it'd fit exactly what he'd have wanted to say if he could have used his own words plainly, but… If he even felt half as much for me as it'd sounded like he did, I didn't know why. How much did he even know me?

Still, the memory resonated through my chest, as if some part of me recognized that emotion, understood it, accepted it. Maybe even longed to return it.

Nothing made sense here, and Jenson really couldn't give me straight answers, even if he wanted to. He stroked his thumb over my cheek so gently, his mouth opening and then closing around things he couldn't say. I closed my eyes for a second in the midst of the feelings rushing through me. Then I eased up on the cot to brush my lips against his.

Jenson's breath stuttered at the kiss. His fingers slid to cup my jaw, easing me in just a little more as he kissed me back—asking rather than demanding.

When I pulled back, his hand dropped, but only to settle on my knee. Something in his eyes had brightened, even if he still looked serious.

"What are you going to do?" he asked, plain and simple.

"I'm not totally sure," I said. It was hard to even think straight through the turmoil that had risen up inside me. "I guess I'll figure it out as I go."

As confused as I might be about everything else, I was more certain than ever of one thing now. I wasn't leaving Roseborne College without a fight.

# CHAPTER TWENTY-FIVE

*Trix*

I headed into the woods at ten past midnight, not wanting to risk missing the time Elias had given me. I didn't remember the exact path Ryo had taken me on earlier in the evening, but my instincts led me onward to where the trees grew closer together and their leaves shut out all but a few scraps of moonlight. Even with the light from my phone, I stubbed my toe on a jutting root and caught a spiderweb across my cheek.

No breeze rustled the leaves tonight. Crickets chirped distantly through the stillness. The cool air seeped under my jacket to trace a chill over my skin. My pulse stuttered at every snap of a twig where some small animal was making its way through the brush.

I wasn't sure what I was going to say or how this would go, but not reaching out simply wasn't an option.

The minutes slipped by on my phone. When the time

flipped over to twelve thirty, I stopped and glanced around. This might have been close to the spot where I'd encountered the monster earlier. I didn't think Ryo and I had walked much longer than twenty minutes. What now?

"Cade?" I called out, and flinched at how loud my voice sounded against the quiet. Well, he'd definitely hear me if he was anywhere nearby. I swiveled on my feet, scanning the darkness beyond the light of my phone, and pitched my voice a little lower. "Cade, it's me."

Another minute passed, and another. My throat started to tighten. Maybe I'd ended up in the wrong part of the woods altogether—maybe I'd miss him and never get this chance again. I shifted my weight, debating whether I should walk farther or call out even louder than before—and the rasp of human footsteps reached my ears.

I turned toward the sound just as a well-built figure with a head of cropped blond hair came into view at the edge of the light, so familiar my heart flipped over. Cade stopped there, still partly cloaked by shadow, and gave me his usual crooked grin, though tonight it was tight around the edges. His hands were slung in the pockets of his jeans, and the wiry muscles in his arms flexed beneath the sleeves of his T-shirt. I'd have thought he'd be freezing in that outfit, but he didn't give any sign of noticing the night's chill.

"Hey, Baby Bea," he said, like it was just another day, like nothing had ever gone wrong.

I choked up even more. I took a step toward him automatically and then balked, torn between wanting to yank him close to confirm he was really there and the uncertainty of whether he'd actually welcome that gesture. Because things had gone wrong, and it'd been a year since I'd seen him. Whether he knew how much I was to blame for that or not, I hadn't been everything he'd wanted for a long time before that too.

He lifted his arms, and that was answer enough. I threw myself into them, embracing him with all the strength in my body. Cade squeezed me back, ducking his head next to mine, the coppery smell of him, exactly as it'd always been, washing over me.

"Of course you'd come," he said with a rough laugh. "Of course you would. You don't let anyone tell you no. This isn't how I wanted you to see me, Trix."

"I couldn't just let you disappear," I mumbled against his shirt. "What they've done to you—it isn't your fault. It doesn't change anything."

"It changes how long we can hold a conversation. There isn't a whole lot of time." He eased back, his hands coming up to frame my face. The pale gray eyes that had stared at me from within that monstrous face just hours ago gazed down at me again in their proper form. "You should fucking despise me and what this place has turned me into."

Every particle in my body resisted that statement. "I know you so much better than they do. You don't belong here at all."

"Are you sure?"

"Of course I am. You only ever got angry at people you had every reason to believe deserved it. You wouldn't have laid into that guy if you hadn't been sure—if it hadn't been for what happened to Sylvie—"

I couldn't bring myself to say more than that. A cold light flashed through Cade's eyes. He wet his lips. "Maybe you were all better off without me."

"*No*," I said, both of my hands clenching where I'd set them against his chest. "Don't you dare believe that. I wouldn't be here if I didn't need you."

"I suppose that could be true." He cocked his head at me. "What are you going to do now that you've found me, Baby Bea? Whether I deserve it or not, I'm still stuck. Nobody can change that."

"You don't know that for sure. I'm still trying to find a way. You've always had my back, and now it's my turn to have yours."

Memories flitted through my mind: that first day at the Fricks when he'd offered me his unconditional friendship, the times he'd tugged me away to the secret spot behind the backyard shed, that careening sled ride when he'd shielded me with his own body from the splintering boards of the fort. The moments in school when he'd threatened classmates who'd ganged up on me, the hours spend lying on one of our beds planning out our joint future with sweeping gestures as if drawing those dreams into being in the air.

"You always said we'd stick together," I added. "So I'm sticking with you. I'm going to take this as far as I can."

"You know I'd never ask you to put yourself on the line for me."

"You don't even need to say that." I gave him a light

shove with my hands, not enough to shift him backward, just to push away that thought.

Did he really think he somehow deserved to be here? All the truth, all the secrets I'd kept tamped down knotted through my chest. I had to say *something* so he'd understand if tonight didn't work out in my favor. What did it matter if he hated me afterward, as long as he didn't hate himself?

How could I really say I'd come all this way for him if I put my fear ahead of his conscience? I'd never really free him if I couldn't admit my part.

I swallowed hard. "You don't know everything about Sylvie. It wasn't really— I should have told you before. I was just so scared of what you'd think of me if you knew. She cared about you just like you cared about her. I should have been happy that you were happy."

"Hey, you don't have to justify anything," Cade said, tucking my hair back behind my ear. "Jealousy comes up. But she could never touch what we had. It was something totally different—a higher level. I'd always have been there for you too."

My eyes went hot. "I believe you. That's why I shouldn't have—" I couldn't stop my head from drooping as I forced the words out. But I had to say it. I *had* to. The night, the forest, the school—as I dragged in my breath, it all seemed to revolve around this moment, this confession.

"I was the one who called her out there to the courtyard that night. The whole idea with the dog and everything was mine. I don't even know—I was going to scare her, and maybe in some weird way I thought she'd go running to you and you'd think she was just silly, that you didn't need her anymore. But mostly I just wanted her to feel like shit for a little while. I never wanted her to get really hurt, let alone— It was so *stupid*."

"Trix," Cade said in a tone I couldn't read. Was he horrified or angry or simply shocked?

I barreled onward before my terror could close my throat. "I didn't know she'd be *that* scared. I let the dog run at her, and she threw herself out of the way so blindly she crashed right into that store—the window—all the glass. By the time I got to her, she was already bleeding so badly… I should have told you. Especially after you figured it was Richie who set up the prank. I should have said something—I should have stopped you—"

"Trix," Cade said again, my name turning thick in his throat. He took a step back, and I glanced up at him, braced for the worst.

He didn't look horrified or angry or shocked—at least, not as much as he was in the grips of something larger. The transformation was coming over him.

Before my eyes, his back had started to hunch, his arms twisting with unnatural joints, his jaw popping forward. Coarse hair sprouted up over his skin. With a hissed curse, the only human speech he seemed capable of in that moment, he swung around and staggered away from me into the shelter of the shadows.

"Cade!" I shouted after him, my voice raw. A shudder ran through me. I wanted to dash after him, but maybe he wouldn't want me near him after what I'd just admitted. Maybe he wouldn't be able to trust himself. He'd pounced on me in his monstrous form before, barely seemed to know who I was. He might be furious now.

And even if he was, he was shielding me like he always had, except this time from himself. Or what the school had twisted him into.

A couple of tears slipped from my eyes to trail cool lines down my cheeks. Had he even had a chance to think through the full implications of what I'd told him? Had he even *heard* the entire story and understood it if the change had been rippling through him before I'd finished?

I couldn't know. He'd warned me there wouldn't be much time. But I'd hesitated too long because I hadn't really wanted to tell him anything, just like I'd let myself swallow down the truth those few weeks right afterward, before Roseborne had claimed him…

I raised my chin, my jaw clenching. I could prove how sorry I was, how much I realized I owed him. God, I owed so many people who'd cared enough to try to help me since I'd arrived here.

Somehow I'd tricked them all into believing I was better than them. There was only one way I could think of to make that true. I'd been brave enough to finally tell Cade the truth—I could be brave enough to do this too.

That mournful moan of a howl rose up from farther away than I'd have expected. I spun and hurried back toward the school, faster now that I wasn't searching the shadows for my brother.

I only slowed when I'd crossed most of the lawn. Coming up the steps to the college building's front door, I set my feet carefully to provoke as little sound as possible.

Not that I was kidding myself that the staff relied only on regular senses. But it seemed better to avoid adding to the things that might catch their attention.

The door murmured open at my push. I slipped into the foyer. My gaze shot straight to the dean's office.

I'd break in like I had before, grab the puzzle box and anything else on the shelves that might contain a key, and if none of them did—well, I'd worry about the rest later.

Except I never got that far.

I'd just turned toward the office, fishing the handy reward card from my pocket, when the door opened for me. Dean Wainhouse stepped out, his expression even more imposing than usual.

I backed up, my heart lurching, and more figures emerged into the other hall from the staff's rooms. Three, then four, then five of the professors moved toward me through the dim space. My gaze jerked from them to the dean and back again from where I'd halted beside one of the suits of armor, my stance gone rigid with tension.

Despite the lack of light, all their faces shone with that silvery sheen I'd noticed on the dean's skin my first day here. They weren't quite human, were they? Maybe not human at all. As they converged around me, I clutched the reward card as if it could offer me any kind of protection.

"It seems you've overstayed your welcome to an even greater extent than we first believed, Miss Corbyn," Dean Wainhouse said. "We've all agreed that it's best if you leave immediately."

I blinked at him. "You want me to take off right now —in the middle of the night."

"Arrangements can still be made. We must do what is best for the school as a whole." He extended his arm and plucked my packed knapsack seemingly straight out of the shadows beside the stairs. "Let's sort this problem out as quickly and efficiently as possible."

My skin crawled as the professors surrounded me. "And if I'd rather wait until the morning like we agreed?"

"Then we'll enforce our decision by whatever means necessary. It'll be much easier for you if you simply accept how this has to be."

*It doesn't* have *to be like this*, I snapped at him in my head. But what could I do with the bunch of them closing in around me? I groped for an answer, for some kind of sign—

And it came with the last of the professors, coming to join the crowd late, the hinges on his door shifting with a creak.

The dry groan echoed through my memory back to the boards of the haphazard fort giving way as my and Cade's sled had slammed into it. With enough speed and enough force, you could break almost anything. The hinges in the secret basement opened inward. Old hinges on an old door. And the huge glinting oval of the empty knight's shield hung right in front of me.

It was a crazy idea. I knew that even as it hit me. But it was an idea, and it was all I had. So I ran with it in the most literal possible way.

I yanked the shield from its place with one hand. With the other, I was already swiveling the card I'd been clutching into the right angle. The heavy slab of metal dragged at my arm with enough weight to make my muscles ache in just a few seconds, but I didn't need much more than that.

One of the staff had already let out a shout of warning. I charged between two of the professors, shoved past the one who was just joining them, and hurtled down the hallway toward the mysterious door at the end.

I'd practiced my trick with the regular locks enough in the last few days that, miraculously, the latch snapped with the first jam of the card against it. The *Bushfell* door flew open. I tossed the shield down on the floor at the top of the stairs and leapt onto it with the full force of my forward momentum.

The shield whipped over the stairs with a clattering that was nearly deafening. I barely managed to keep my balance on it with the heave of it passing each step, my fingers gripping the hand holds. But it sped faster and faster as it raced downward. My target, the padlocked door at the bottom, seemed to rush toward me more quickly than I'd been prepared for. I clenched my fingers tighter and squeezed my eyes shut.

The shield slammed into the door so hard my bones rattled against each other. The padlock held—but the hinges on the other side popped. The wrong end of the door jolted open just far enough for me to scramble off the shield and stumble through the gap, ignoring a growing throbbing in my head and the smack of my shoulder against the frame.

Frantic feet pounded down the stairs after me. I dashed down the grim gray hallway, skidded and spun at a bend, and threw myself onward into a yawning room at its end.

A few strides into the room, I teetered to a halt, caught between the headache splintering deeper into my skull and the bewildering scene before me. My legs threatened to buckle.

At my entrance, sconces set in the concrete walls had glowed to life with an unearthly glow. Their light wavered across a row of eight photographs fixed to the wall beside me beneath names gouged into the concrete. School photographs: eight students in the same maroon uniforms as in the painted portraits upstairs.

The light also caught on dark crimson splotches that marked the floor here and there like pools of dried blood. Or not just *like* but the real thing. A rancid metallic scent laced the air, alongside a pungent rose scent so thick it was almost liquid. Normally I liked the smell of roses, but this was so overpoweringly heady it turned my stomach.

Which was strange, even though the most eerie thing in the room was the gnarled rosebush that loomed from a hole in the center of the concrete floor. It took up nearly half of the space in the room with its dark, twisted brambles, but I didn't see a single flower blooming between the leaves and the thorns as long as my hand and as sharp as daggers.

No, something different clung here and there on the brambles. A scrap of ragged leather. A single dingy shoelace. A ripped, yellowed paper printed with lines of type. Was that thing over there a gnarled *toenail?*

And just beside it hung a tangled lock of rich red hair, the exact same shade as Delta's.

I didn't want to stand any closer to that monstrosity of a plant than I already was, but my pursuers had nearly caught up with me. I darted around the bush, searching for another hall or some tool I could use. The other side of the room offered me nothing.

The seven figures of the staff filed into the room, forming a solid barrier between me and the one doorway. A hum coursed through the air, power so potent I could taste it like electricity on my tongue.

Professor Hubert let out a low laugh. "You think you've accomplished something by getting this far? We were giving you a way out, and you've thrown it away. Don't imagine that will ever happen again."

"She never learns," Professor Roth remarked. "Over and over again in the same cycle, spinning her wheels, until we send her right back to where she started."

Back to where I'd started? Over and over again? I eyed him from where I stood tensed beside the twisted rosebush. "What are you talking about?"

"Do you really think you're in control of any of this?" Dean Wainhouse asked. "We might not have called you here, but we make use of what we have. You've provided plenty of torment we couldn't have dreamed up on our own for the student body. Arriving here again and again, asking the same ridiculous questions, making a fool of yourself like you always do, until we decide it's time to return you to the beginning. You have no idea how many times you've taken your little stands and made your meager protests, and they've never gotten you anywhere. You saw today how sick your classmates are of it."

A queasy sort of understanding seeped through my mind. I'd done this before? All the progress I'd made, it was only a hopeless repeat of things I'd tried in some other attempt I couldn't remember?

It could be true. With powers like they had, why wouldn't they be able to wipe my mind of any memory of being here before, toss me back to the gate as if I'd only just arrived?

How many times had I gone through those motions while they looked on with the amusement that shone on their faces now? Horror wound through my chest.

No wonder the other students had seemed so annoyed with me. No wonder Ryo and Jenson and Elias had responded to my presence as if they already knew what to make of me before they'd had any chance to meet me. *You remind me of someone else*, Elias had said, and maybe he'd meant another me I couldn't recall.

My head pounded, and my stomach balled. But through the nausea and the revulsion, my mind latched onto Professor Hubert's words.

I'd gotten far this time. They didn't normally try to send me away. It hadn't happened before. Maybe I'd retraced my steps without knowing it a dozen times before, but I didn't think I'd ever made it all the way to this room and the most vital evidence of their wicked power. The rosebush beside me vibrated with it. A manifestation of that power? Its source?

Either way, energy flowed between the plant and

them, just like it must each of the students and their roses along the wall outside. The bush, the blood, the photographs on the wall—they added up to some kind of answer. I just didn't have the time to piece it together.

"You came to us," Dean Wainhouse said, stepping closer, "and you'll have your curse like the rest of them. We'll just keep throwing you back until it breaks you."

He raised his hands, and a bolt of panic shot through me. They were going to do it again—steal my memories, send me back to the beginning with no clue I'd ever been here before. No clue where Cade was. No clue what three guys, whom as far as I would know I'd never met, had done for me.

No fucking way.

The bush's thorns glinted like razors in the eerie glow. If that thing had power, then why couldn't I call on it too? Give it more than just a token of who I was.

Shatter myself like the window in my memories, cut myself open like those shards of glass had cut into Sylvie. It would be perfectly fitting. Payment for my crimes and a sort of absolution.

A twinge of regret tingled through my heart. Ryo. Jenson. Elias. This wasn't the fate any of them had wanted for me. But they hadn't known the full story. They couldn't know what I needed to do to make everything right.

They'd wanted me safe. So I'd do this for them too. I'd break, but let's see how much I could break with me. With one crack opened, the whole school might fall apart.

The dean's hands wove through the air. The thrum of

power started to swirl around me. I eased back a step to give myself a running start.

"I'm not really yours," I said, letting my voice peal through the room. "But I give myself on one condition. Take me, and let Cade Harrison go."

Then I hurled myself at the densest patch of thorns.

Someone yelled. Pain sliced through me. In the back of my head, that one thought stayed with me as a fog rolled over the rest.

They'd wanted me safe. In spite of everything, three men I knew and yet didn't had committed themselves to saving me.

A glimmer of warmth lit in my chest, and then a dark fog rolled through me, wiping everything away.

# CHAPTER TWENTY-SIX

*Trix*

The gate closed behind me, the wrought-iron bars clanging shut with a finality that made my nerves jump. I glanced back, half expecting to see chains and padlocks had magically sprung up to seal my way out.

It still looked as ridiculously foreboding as before, tall and black with imperious twists rising along the arched top, but no unexpected barriers had sprung up. I studied it a moment longer anyway. My hand closed at my side, and a sudden prickle of pain jerked my gaze downward.

The thin red lines of open scratches covered my right palm. Scratches that formed letters and then words when I stared at them.

*They wanted me safe.*

I blinked and read the sentence again. With an itch that dug deep into my skin, the scratches started to fade away. In a matter of seconds, my palm looked as unmarked as I'd have expected, although a thin pang of discomfort remained.

The growl of the cab's engine was fading beyond the thick stone wall. Up ahead of me loomed a sprawling Victorian mansion. The smell of roses saturated the air. And memories tickled up through my head.

Somewhere ahead of me were three young men who'd all looked at me as if I were some kind of answer: Ryo with his punk-green hair and gentle affection, Jenson with his off-kilter nose and barbed charm, Elias with his deep brown eyes and rigid confidence. There would be classes that dredged up the worst out of us, whether through words or vomit. And in the woods lurked a beast that hid a young man inside it.

More and more of the impressions flooded my mind, piecing together into a patchwork quilt that stretched back weeks upon weeks, moments layered on moments, until I could hardly breathe. But even as my lungs constricted, I stared up at the school building with growing resolve ringing through me.

I knew who I was. I knew what I was doing here. Whatever I'd done last time, it might have saved not just Cade but every other student here—and me—after all. Because this time I remembered, and I'd be damned if I let the fiends that ran Roseborne College stop me again.

Eva Chase lives in Canada with her family. She loves stories both swoony and supernatural, and strong women and the men who appreciate them. Along with the Cursed Studies trilogy, she is the author of the Royals of Villain Academy series, the Moriarty's Men series, the Looking Glass Curse trilogy, the Their Dark Valkyrie series, the Witch's Consorts series, the Dragon Shifter's Mates series, the Demons of Fame Romance series, the Legends Reborn trilogy, and the Alpha Project Psychic Romance series.

*Connect with Eva online:*
www.evachase.com
eva@evachase.com